Praise for The Warrior Teenager

Through real-life stories, Mary Lynne gives a peek into the teen psyche and shows teenagers that they are not alone when they feel overwhelmed, stressed, and confused about life. She breaks down a wealth of information into a practical step-by-step plan so they can take action to create a life of strength, confidence and ultimately a life of happiness.

— Harriet Turk, Professional Speaker and Author of *After The Speech: When Teens Get Real.*

Mary Lynne's book, "The Warrior Teenager," is the perfect book for teenagers who are struggling with depression, suicidal thoughts, feelings of hopelessness and despair. Every chapter is weaved with analogies and captivating stories that create rich visual images in the reader's mind. Each story is grounded in practical strategies for teenagers to empower and transform their lives.

— Janet Bray Attwood, NY Times Bestselling Author of *The Passion Test* and *Your Hidden Riches.*

I do not know how Mary Lynne Fernandez packed such a fantastic amount of inspiration and insight into her book, "The Warrior Teenager." Any teen who reads this book is definitely going to benefit from its wisdom. A new standard has been set.

— Ray Lozano, Drug & Substance Prevention Specialist, and Youth Speaker

As a mother of two teenagers, I highly recommend reading "The Warrior Teenager" to all parents of teenagers. Mary Lynne has effectively translated her challenges, experiences, awareness, and wisdom into an awe-inspiring guide with practical strategies for today's youth. This is an excellent work of hope and confidence that helps young adults rise to become the Warrior Teenager in their lives.

— Gagan Sarkaria, High Achievement Wellness & Business Coach | The Branding Expert

I applaud author Mary Lynne Fernandez's commitment to helping teens overcome self-sabotage and gain back their power. Her life experiences and self-discoveries in the book, "The Warrior Teenager," are super impactful. She teaches teens to become warriors, so they do not suffer the heartache of being a wounded child after reaching adulthood. Mary Lynne courageously embraces her vulnerability and beautifully presents her knowledge and successful strategies to the teens and their parents.

— JohnEgreek, Award Winning and Bestselling Author of *Grandma's Secret Blessings: A Memoir with a Twist*

"Mary Lynne Fernandez has written a manual of hope and courage with specific suggestions that will be of immediate assistance to teenagers and their parents."

— *Barbara H. Reed, Author of Rx For Recidivism*

THE *Warrior* TEENAGER

Let Go of Self-Sabotage & Embrace Your True Power

Mary Lynne Fernandez
International, LLC

The Warrior Teenager
Let Go of Self-Sabotage & Embrace Your True Power

Personal Branding Expert: Gagan Sarkaria, MFA, MBA.
Cover Designers: Gagan Sarkaria & Abbey Wilkerson: www.UnfoldYour Success.com
Author photo by Beth Sanders at www.BethPhotography.com
Typography: Antonio Bold, Messy Script, Anziano

ISBN 978-0-9840031-2-9 - paperback

E-book ISBN 978-0-9840031-3-6 – ebook

Fernandez, Mary Lynne
The warrior teenager: let go of self-sabotage and embrace your true power / Mary Lynne Fernandez.
1. Teenagers - Life Skills guides 2. Teenagers - Conduct of Life 3. Interpersonal relations in adolescence
I. Title

Warning - Disclaimer
The sole purpose of this book is to educate and entertain. There is no guarantee made by the author or publisher that anyone following the ideas, tips, techniques, or suggestions will become successful. The author and publisher have neither liability nor responsibility to anyone with respect to any loss or damage caused, or alleged to be caused, directly or indirectly by the information contained in this book.

In order to respect the anonymity of all individuals mentioned in this book, identities, names, and certain details have been modified. All stories are told from the author's perspective and experience at that time in her life.

*The author is fully aware that "depleter" is not a real word. She uses the word "depleter" to mean a person, place, or thing that depletes one's power.

To Pedro
*Thank you for making me laugh, your love,
and continual support.*

In Memory of my Gram
*Thank you for lighting up my life with your smile, phone
calls, letters, and chocolate chip cookies!*

To Coco & Nina, my writing pals & officemates
*Thanks for your spontaneous barking, staring me down
when it's dinner-time, our many snuggles,
and endless kisses.*

Contents

A Warrior Teenager

— One who overcomes personal pain and suffering through the use of one's own True Power

1

Response to Reality

Suicide

"One who gains strength by overcoming obstacles possesses the only strength which can overcome adversity." — Albert Schweitzer

The sun shone through the faint curtains as I opened my eyes. Quick to re-close them, I buried my face into my feather pillow. I lay there wearing a tank top and boxer shorts, my stomach flat on the firm mattress, covered with a light sheet.

Hearing a neighbor mowing a lawn in the distance, I smelled the fresh-cut grass. I turned my head to the right, peering out from underneath the sheet: 10:13 AM gleamed in red on my clock radio. I turned my head the other way, curling my body into a small ball, covering my whole self with the sheet. Feeling the heat from the summer sun, I opened my eyes.

A warm feeling stirred within me, "Must be Dad's not home," I thought. If he was, heavy footsteps, an abrupt opening of my bedroom door, and a stern "Get up!" would have been my wake-up call. Even during the summer, he didn't let me sleep in. There was always work to be done: mowing the gigantic lawn, driving the tractor at the farm, weeding, feeding the calves, vacuuming, dusting, whatever.

Today was soundless and tranquil.

I whipped the sheets off me, turned to my left, and shimmied to the side of the bed. Swinging my legs around, I sat up and planted my feet on the floor, glancing into the opened closet in front of me. I surveyed the room for what to wear. Noticing the pile of clothes at the foot of my bed, I decided to wear what I had on yesterday.

Stepping over last month's Seventeen magazine and white cordless phone, I made my way to the large, pearl white framed mirror at the front of the room, the only thing remaining from my childhood bedroom set. The gray carpet felt cushy on my bare feet.

The summer breeze greeted me as I felt it on the back of my neck and arms. Flowing from the two corner windows, I turned to see the white curtains dancing in the air. Already feeling the hot August sun, I walked across the room and pushed down on the three-foot wide windows, one by one.

Making my way back to the door, I wondered if anyone was home.

I opened the door, walked down the hall, past the basement door on my right, and came to the archway of the kitchen. As I turned to my right, my heart skipped a beat, my body swayed backward, teetering between the soft, carpeted hallway and the hard, cold linoleum kitchen floor. My wide green eyes glanced in front of me as my chin lowered. There he was, my dad, sitting at the kitchen table reading the local newspaper.

"That's weird," I thought.

I had known my dad only for seventeen years, but he seemed to always look the same, a beer belly and brush cut. Sometimes he'd come home smelling like manure, other times like the bar. Neither today.

My teeth clenched, as I put my head down and entered. No "good morning," nod, nothing. That was normal and welcomed at this point.

Our kitchen was small. The rectangular brown and white chrome-plated table was in the center with three chairs around it. The broken dishwasher, topped with papers and odd-stuff, sat where the fourth chair used to be, where I used to sit when my brother lived with us. Now I was an only child; it had been seven years since my brother moved to Grandma's house, then went to college.

I maneuvered my way between the back of my dad's chair and the kitchen counter. Opening the bottom brown cupboard, I perused my choices: Wheaties, Special K, Raisin Bran, Total. Sometimes Fruity Pebbles or Fruit Loops would be hidden in the back, but only when my mom would allow it.

I don't really understand why I couldn't have sugared cereal since I had a snack drawer full of Doritos, Cheetos, Twinkies, Cupcakes, Ho-Ho's, and Oatmeal Creme Pies. We called it the "junk drawer" for good reason.

Playing it safe, I grabbed the Wheaties and set the box on the white and brown speckled counter top.

In front of me, against the powder blue painted wall, was our old brown box radio, three inches wide, twelve inches long, and ten inches tall - not on.

I opened both top cupboard doors in front of me and grabbed a white bowl from the stack on the first shelf then pulled out the drawer from underneath and picked a spoon from the pile in the middle.

As I opened the Wheaties, my nose scrunched from the strong whiff of wheat. Pouring about a half bowl full, I simultaneously reached for the small white bowl in front of the radio, bringing it closer to me. Taking off the lid, I scooped a couple spoonsful of sugar onto my Wheaties and pushed the sugar bowl back, leaving the opened Wheaties box to take care of later.

I pulled open the white refrigerator door on my right. On the lower shelf was the milk. I reached forward with both hands, sure to use my legs, and lifted the large glass jar, placing it on the counter. Why couldn't we be like everyone else and buy our milk at the Big M? A simple carton of milk would be much easier than a gallon jug weighing a ton!

Full of light white liquid and about an inch of cream, I shook the full gallon jar watching the cream disperse, like snowflakes floating in the wind. I twisted the white metal lid off, placed it on the counter, and picked up the glass jug, pouring fresh-from-the-cow milk onto my cereal. Milk bounced off the top layer of crisp wheat flakes, splattering all around the bowl. Finally ready, I turned around and made my way to my chair, adjacent to my dad.

With my head down, I focused on my cereal, circulating the milk with my spoon and submerging all of the wheat flakes. Finally, I lifted a spoonful of slightly moist and crunchy flakes into my mouth. Mmmmm … I just love the taste of cold milk and sugar. That's what makes the cereal taste so good. I stared straight in front of me, noticing the bright cobalt-blue sky out the kitchen window.

The newspaper crinkled as he turned the page.

I looked back down and took another bite. The crunch between my teeth thundered in the surrounding silence.

From behind the newspaper, my dad mumbled something, words that were incomprehensible. "Your buddy killed himself last night."

Stopping mid-bite, my eyes squinted and my head tilted to the right so my right ear could tune in on his words once more.

"Huh?" I asked, dumbfounded.

He lowered the newspaper, looked straight at me and said, "The Connelly boy killed himself last night," so matter-of-factly it pissed me off. I waited for him to take it back like I was in kindergarten or something. He just sat there.

My stomach curled and my throat clenched as I swallowed the cereal. I wanted to cry but didn't. I dropped my spoon in my cereal and ran to my room, shutting the door behind me. Tears began to flow down my face as my heart pounded. I gasped for air. My face was drenched with moisture. Wiping the snot from my nose, I circled the room, scanning the carpet for answers.

Feeling the perspiration under my arms, I asked myself, "Is it true? Is it true? It can't be true!"

Looking up, I saw my boom box in the corner, sitting on a flimsy TV stand with cassette tapes stacked in front of it. I rushed over to it and pushed the gray plastic switch away from me with my index finger, past TAPE PLAYER to RADIO.

Mitch's soothing voice vibrated from the round mesh speakers, calming me for just one second. His next words answered my endless questioning, "You'll be missed, our friend."

The Steve Miller Band song, *Jetliner*, followed, echoing out in honor of our mutual friend.

In that moment, I knew it was true.

That's the kind of moment you think will never happen to you. It's something that happens to other people in other towns, in other cities, in other parts of the world, but not in yours, not in mine, never. But it did.

It's moments like that, that alter the way you view life. For me, it was the moment I realized I didn't want to die, I didn't want to end my life. I had thought about it every year for several years, thinking to myself that it would get better, it would be different, and yet, I'm not sure if it ever really did.

We all have moments in life that stick in our minds forever, but after that day, I never again considered ending my life. Life hasn't been easy, it's had its ups and downs, but I've kept going, kept trying, and most importantly, kept learning how to help myself, how to love myself, and how to live in this world.

What are the moments in your life that stick out for you? That make you feel good, bad, whatever? How have they influenced you? How will you keep going, keep trying, and keep learning?

Squashed by a Cow

"You don't need to or should not feel like a victim ... nobody can help you more than you can help yourself. — Lady Gaga

My grandparents' dairy farm was where I spent a lot of my childhood; playing with recently born calves and puppies, ice skating on the pond, playing with the neighbors up the road, and just roaming around the barn.

The aroma of manure didn't seem to faze me, but the smell of chewing tobacco sure did. Every day, Grandpa would stand with his shoulders hunched forward and pull out a white plastic-like pouch with a picture of an Indian on it from the left front pocket of his army-green shirt. It was Big Red Chewing Tobacco.

He'd unroll it using both hands, then separate the two sides. Placing it in his left hand, he'd reach his right index finger and thumb inside, grab about an inch of brown stringy stuff and place it in his left side cheek, gnawing on it for hours.

Grandpa must have been tired of me asking what it tasted like because one day he told me to stand next to him for a minute. He reached in his Big Red pouch, took a smidge, and glanced three feet down, seeing the excitement in my nickel-sized eyes.

Placing my right hand underneath my left, I eagerly awaited the free gift.

Soon, a wee bit of brown stringy stuff was laid upon my opened hand. I dropped my head down staring at it, taking a couple sniffs. I took my right hand from underneath and, just like Grandpa, I picked up that little smidge of tobacco and placed it in my mouth.

My neck instantaneously leaned back, my nose scrunched up as my eyebrows compressed together. My mouth formed an upside-down U. "Yuck!" I shrieked as I spit it out onto the white concrete floor in front of me.

The smoky, vinegary flavor was still on my tongue as I continued to spit and spat. My grandpa, usually soundless and hunched over, straightened up, tilted his head back and let out one of the few laughs I ever heard from him.

You and I both have memories and stories from childhood. Our parents tell us stories all the time, some we know and remember - like that one for me - and some we're too young to remember. Some are funny, some not, and some are meant to totally embarrass us, while others are just plain unbelievable.

The bright sun illuminated the sky above as my brother and I, wearing black rubber boots up to our knees, roamed around the smooth, concrete floor, pouncing in the water that lay accumulated at the foot of the soapy black and white cow standing in front of us. I was two, my brother was six. My dad, water hose in hand, stood close to the cow. He covered the rushing water at the head of the hose with his thumb, buffering the force.

Water cascaded down the cow, suds of soap leading the way as the cold water followed. Soon, a lake of sudsy swirls surrounded the fifteen-hundred-pound cow, forming a perfect playground.

I pounced close by, in hopes of a bigger splash. The concrete floor soon became too slick for the four hooves that stood upon it. The cow's legs began to tap dance on the water like a dancing puppet. Finally, the cow landed flat on the slate, making the biggest splash of all – with me underneath!

Obviously, I survived the fall and, surprisingly, never was hospitalized or hurt. How? I have no idea. I guess luck was on my side that day.

But, I wonder if that cow falling on me was a metaphor for my life. I mean, really, it seems like I've been squashed by a lifetime's worth of limiting thoughts, beliefs, and self-sabotage. I've literally spent the majority of my life making myself miserable with the stories I made up in my head, comparing myself to others, telling myself lies, and not enjoying life to its fullest.

What about you? Do you have stories that are hidden metaphors for your life?

We all have problems, dilemmas, issues, drama, you name it. I want you to know that you aren't alone. I always thought I was the only one, but I've come to realize that I'm not and neither are you.

We're surrounded by teachers and mentors in life, people that guide and influence our lives, but the best kinds of teachers are the ones who are still learning and owning their stuff. They are the ones who are real; who are beside you to learn, to share, and to live.

Not only do you have teachers in your life, but you are a teacher to others, too. We are all here to help and guide each other to live lives worthy of living, full of joy and laughter.

Our minds can create stories that bring us up or take us down. We can blame our circumstances and the people around us, or we can decide to be the change we want in our lives. I figured out how to be the answer for my own problems and you can, too. In this book, I'll show you how. Together, we can do this!

Death & Loss

"We're still building and burning down love, burning down love. And when I go there, I go there with you, it's all I can do." — U2

My mom had black hair with a white stripe that streamed from right to left an inch above her forehead. Sitting at the kitchen table, she giggled at the comic section of the local newspaper. School seemed far away, it being the second week into summer vacation.

Finished, she closed the pages together, folded it in half, and placed it face up in the center of the cleared table. Pointing to the front page, she looked at me stating, "Tragic. Just tragic. I don't know what they were thinking." She pushed her chair back, stood up, and walked out to the living room.

I reached for the newspaper, and examined the headline, Two Teenagers Die – Reckless Driving. My chest raised as I let out a deep sigh. Curious to know what happened, I began to read the details. One paragraph in, I raised my head and peered above the kitchen sink through the blue and white plaid curtained window. As I squinted, I located the location of the accident in my head.

"That's just down the road!" I thought silently to myself.

Reaching above my head with my right hand, I picked up the receiver from the white rectangular phone on the wall and brought it down to my ear, balancing it between my left shoulder and head. I reached back up, twisting my body around to see, and dialed 7-digits, hearing each number click repeatedly in my ear.

I waited patiently for Daphne, D for short, to pick up. Finally, after the seventh ring, she answered. I briefly told her about the accident and asked if she wanted to go check it out with me. She agreed.

I found my mom and asked if it was okay if I went to D's house to play. She replied, "Yes, but be home for dinner."

Walking out the front door, I found my turquoise bike leaning against the house on the front porch. I grabbed the right soiled handgrip and pulled the bike up next to me. As I walked to the driveway, I noticed Mr. Brady across the street weeding. Bending my right knee, I stepped through to the other side, finding the plastic pedal. I maneuvered my butt onto the seat, pushed off with my left toes and coasted down the short hill of a driveway.

Mr. Brady looked up, smiled, and waved. I waved back as I turned to the right, pedaling past our mailbox and the tall round pine tree. The scent of chlorine from their pool rolled through the warm June air as I continued down the street past five more houses to the end. Gazing to the left, I glided through the stop sign and went right. I spied D on her bike riding across her yard and made a u-ey. She soon caught up to me.

We continued to ride down the charcoal-colored paved road, outlined with broken edges and piles of pebbles. Black squiggly marks sporadically lined the road as cracks ran from side to side. Pedaling past an open field on our right, I observed three horses standing in the corner, grazing on a pile of fresh golden hay.

We came to a four-way corner with a two-story, white, square house on the right, covered in vines and overgrown weeds. A stale black rectangular sign stood tall in the front yard. Oldest House in Sterling County stood out in raised tarnished tangerine lettering. We slowed down and looked up "the ramp" to see if any cars were coming. Nope. We turned to the right.

Pedaling down the middle of the road, I accelerated down the slight decline, hearing the trickle of the river close by. As I hit the green iron bridge, my feet lifted slightly from the pedals, and both hands jiggled as they loosely encircled the handgrips. I leaned to the right, tilted my chin downward, feeling the slight strain and warmth of the sun on my lengthened neck. My eyes looked down through the thick iron lattice and watched the water ripple below, feeling the coolness on my face.

The sense of freshness disappeared quickly as my view turned to brown gravel. I impulsively swung my body back up, put my feet on the pedals, and grasped the handlebars. My bike and body vibrated over the rough earth as I searched for a smoother line. I looked ahead. A half-mile of lofty trees made a cave-like covering, shading the entire ride.

D and I were on a mission. Our eyes met and we both smiled.

Suddenly, her smile disappeared as she looked behind. My eyes followed.

A car! She went to the left side, I went to the right. The car ripped by with windows down and music blaring. A thick cloud of dust followed, swallowing us whole. My face dropped, covering my eyes with my right hand. I coughed and heard D coughing, too. We slowed down and waited for the dust to settle.

Before long, the hovering tree line ended and a window of sunlight beamed between the puffy white clouds. We stopped in the middle of the road and scanned the area full circle, I heard nothing but a couple birds singing in the distance. A dusty, narrow paved road sat to our left, railroad tracks straight ahead, and a field of tall golden grass and scattered young trees to our right.

Discovering two matted-down paths through the tall golden grass, we got off our bikes, walked to the side of the road and laid them gently down on their sides, hearing the scrunch of the grass beneath. D walked down one path, I walked down the other, stepping over and around mutilated baby trees, not yet large enough to survive the impact of a 3,000-pound car.

Ultimately, I came to a foot-wide light brown tree trunk at the end of the path. Examining it, I noticed a gash in its bark, exposing the light interior with a brush stroke of red down the middle, blood one day old.

Days later, I continued to feel the pain and sadness of the deceased teenager's family and friends without even knowing them. It's sad when we lose someone, whether we know them or not.

This was the result of driving recklessly and making spontaneous decisions without taking time to think first. We're all out to have fun and accidents happen, but sometimes they can lead to serious injuries and even death, like this one.

You have a choice to make in each and every moment. There's not much for me to say except to slow down and think before you act. Your life matters, your choices matter, and we need you.

The Importance of Mourning

"So long as the memory of certain beloved friends lives in my heart, I shall say that life is good."
— Helen Keller

The loud music blared from the black speakers surrounding the stage and theatre. Every seat in the balcony, mezzanine, and orchestra levels had someone sitting in it. Eyes widened as dancers flew through the air, hands whipped back and forth as the girl in the middle spun on her head. The audience roared in response to the heightened energy.

This celebration was the most amazing event I had ever been to in honor of someone. It mimicked the life that was physically missing, but still remained in our hearts. I was honored to put together a slideshow of photos and music for the event. And, although it was sad, we got to honor and celebrate my close friend for who she was and what she brought to our lives.

In days after, a group of friends and I got together to pay homage to our dear friend. We went on a short hike in the mountains, blew bubbles in the air, and shared loving memories together. We laughed, we cried, we connected, and we held each other up in honor of her.

Friends and acquaintances of mine have died from drunk driving, fatal accidents, and illnesses - even cancer.

Growing up, we never talked about it. I never knew how to handle those kinds of things. I was never really taught what to do or what to say and I'm definitely not an expert, but I've learned how important it is to mourn the loss of someone you care about - and to talk about it.

The act of mourning used to be normally accepted in society. Some people feel you should move on with your life quicker than you may want to or are ready to. Figure out what's right for you and listen to your heart. Give yourself time to mourn their loss in whatever way is best for you.

Talking is good. Crying is good. Celebrating is good, and supporting yourself and others is good, too.

Suicide is Not the Answer

"And I know, it's hard when you're falling down and it's a long way up when you hit the ground, but get up now, get up, get up now."
— Imagine Dragons, *On Top of the World* song lyrics

Thoughts love to take over our minds. It's all good if those thoughts are full of love and happiness but, if those thoughts bring you down, make you doubt yourself, or are fear driven, then it's the Ego Mind in the driver's seat, bringing pain and struggle to your life.

As I said earlier, I had suicidal thoughts when I was a teenager. It was like I had a split personality; I was happy with my friends, but then I'd go home and not want to be there. Life can be difficult and you can feel like you're the only one going through whatever you're going through, but everyone's got stuff they're dealing with — whether they say it or show it or not.

Anxiety, depression, and worry are all fear-based emotions that get in the way of loving ourselves. Fear is the root cause of depression, which causes a person to doubt the goodness of life so much they want to end it. According to the Centers for Disease and Control and Prevention, suicide is the third leading cause of death for youth between the ages of 10 and 24[1].

Know that every problem has a solution. Obsessive thoughts may get you down and make you feel as if there isn't one, but if you breathe and trust that you will be taken care of, you will be. Problems will pass, things will get better, and life will go on. Suicide is not the answer.

Throughout this book, I give ways to help yourself. Pick and choose what works for you and share them with your friends if you want to. If you have other ways that you use, that work for you, let me know. I'd love to share them with others. I believe that we are all here to get through life the best way we can and to help each other along the way.

Signs of Depression

"Bad things do happen; how I respond to them defines my character and the quality of my life. I can choose to sit in perpetual sadness, immobilized

---

[1] https://www.cdc.gov/healthcommunication/toolstemplates/
entertainmented/tips/suicideyouth.html

by the gravity of my loss, or I can choose to rise from the pain and treasure the most precious gift I have - life itself." — Walter Anderson

My heart fluttered as if it had been awakened from a deep sleep. I was in awe of the vulnerability of the speakers and audience members as they conversed so openly about their personal issues.

A teenager stood at the podium sharing her story of depression; a parent, whose child died by suicide, spoke of her heart-breaking experience; and afterwards, a panel of experts contributed their knowledge of depression and suicide with the audience.

I left that event in a state of confusion, questioning my past, "Does that mean I was depressed all those years?"

I never even considered it. I mean, depressed people walk around like zombies, moping all the time, and locked up in their rooms, right?

At some point in my life, I could have easily fit the category and yet in the rural area I grew up in, I never even heard the word depression. No one was depressed, everyone was fine. No one would ever speak to a counselor or therapist of any kind. You just didn't do that. I don't even know if they existed.

But here I was, in my new community, listening to local high schoolers speak so eloquently about their feelings, their emotions, what it was like for them and how they got help. It was a whole new world for me. I learned what depression really was and the signs of depression and suicide.

I know it's not new information, but how was it new to me?

My purpose for writing this book is to provide a go-to guide to help navigate the ups and downs of life. There is so much going on in this world, I can't possibly include every topic, but I tried to get the basics, the root of self-sabotage and how to help yourself through it. Besides sharing personal stories with you, I also want to give you information.

Below are signs to look for if you or someone you know seem depressed.

Warning Signs of Depression[2]:

- Feeling sad, hopeless, or irritable a lot of the time
- Not wanting to do or enjoy doing fun things
- Changes in eating patterns – eating a lot more or a lot less than usual
- Changes in sleep patterns – sleeping a lot more or a lot less than normal
- Changes in energy – being tired and sluggish or tense and restless a lot of the time
- Having a hard time paying attention
- Feeling worthless, useless, or guilty
- Self-injury and self-destructive behavior

---

[2] http://www.cdc.gov/childrensmentalhealth/depression.html# depression

According to the National Institute of Mental Health, in order to be diagnosed with depression, symptoms such as the warning signs listed must be present for at least two weeks[3].

Looking at those signs, I definitely could have checked off most of them when I was a teenager, but then no one knew it and if they did, they didn't know what to do about it.

There's a wide spectrum of what defines depression. Those on the highest level of the spectrum definitely should consult a professional for help. For minor cases, which I believe was the case for me, owning my stuff and continuing to learn and grow as a person really helped.

"I think that everything is possible as long as you put your mind to it and put the work and time into it."
— Michael Phelps

Life can definitely have struggles, but it is doable and it is worth it. People become depressed when they look outside themselves for answers and compare themselves to others. I know it sounds weird, but doing your own self-work and finding your True Power, your inner strength, is the only way. It hasn't been easy and there are moments when I still doubt and question life, but that's when I know I have to keep going.

All you have to do is get back to you, the inner you, the Real You - and love who you are. You have dreams and

---

[3] https://www.nimh.nih.gov/health/topics/depression/index.shtml

you can make those dreams happen. Your life matters, your choices matter, and we need you - just as you are!

Crazy Mind vs. Calm Mind

"Before you react, think. Before you quit, try. Before you criticize, wait." — Unknown

An average brain weighs about three pounds. Three pounds — that's it! Your brain contains your mind. Your mind contains thousands and thousands of thoughts, memories, and information.

Your mind can be calm or it can be chaotic.

It can be busy with thoughts spiraling out of control — which makes you spiral out of control. Or, it can be calm, leaving you in a calm state.

Think of a time when you felt like you were going crazy — maybe it was because of the people around you, a text you received, or something going on in your life; whatever it was, it spiraled you out of control, making you feel like you were crazy.

It reminds me of a cat playing with a ball of yarn. The yarn is like your brain, bouncing back and forth; up, down, and all around, making you feel crazy and really dizzy. This craziness that you feel started in your mind as a result of the thoughts that you think.

That crazy mind also influences your decision making. When you don't slow down and think, realizing that your crazy mind is leading the way, you can react instantaneously, sometimes with regret.

Maybe you read a text and freak out (crazy mind) then you text back (not stopping to think first — making a spontaneous decision) and push send. Thirty-seconds later, you freak out again, realizing you should not have said what you said. That's your crazy mind making decisions which result in more chaos and stress for you ... ugh!

Then there is the calm mind. The calm mind is like floating in the water or lounging on the couch. You're relaxed and able to think clearly. Your thoughts are calm, strong, and solid. You know you're making the best decision and choice for you in that moment.

These thoughts come from your calm mind. They are based on something you feel deep within that helps you make decisions and choices that are aligned with your life values and dreams you have for yourself. They feel good.

Have you ever made a decision that you know was the right one for you? You didn't second-guess yourself or have to get anyone's opinion? You just knew. That's your calm mind in action.

What about when you make a choice, then incessantly obsess over it wondering if it was the best one for you or not? That's your crazy mind taking over.

When someone drinks and drives, they're almost never using their calm mind. It's just like texting without thinking — it's your crazy mind making choices and decisions and you're not even aware of what you're doing in that moment.

It only takes a second to stop and think before making decisions, and acting on them. Maybe take a minute to breathe, walk away, get in the present moment, and ask yourself, "What's the best thing I could do right now?"

That will trigger your calm mind to take over and help figure things out.

How to Align for Answers:

1. Relax
2. Breathe
3. Tune-in
4. Ask
5. Listen
6. Receive
7. Trust

When you slow down, you will be directed more by your calm mind — making decisions and choices that feel good to you and ultimately create less stress and drama in your life. Yay!

"Happiness can be found even in the darkest of times, if one only remembers to turn on the light."
— Dumbledore, *Harry Potter and the Prisoner of Azkaban*

2

False Realities

Assumptions & Judgments

"We have to keep in mind that we are learners, not judges." — Father Laurence

I had been in India for three weeks. With one day remaining, I was determined to find small gifts for my thirty-two English as a Second Language students back home. I journeyed across the walking bridge from one side of the Ganges River to the other. A honey-brown cow stood on the right and two peanut-colored monkeys sat on the railing made of rope on the left. I maneuvered my way around the cow, trailing behind the line of people, the murky water flowing below.

Once on the other side, I stopped at the first table I came to. The man in front of me wore an indigo v-neck sweater with a maroon tie underneath. His raven black hair was greased smoothly to the left side. Just like the statue of Krishna across the river, he stood calmly in silence, eyes open wide.

I asked him the cost of the items in front of me and was met with no reply. I asked again. Then, I tried acting out what I wanted. Nothing worked.

Turning my head to the right, I noticed we had an audience. A man and woman sat next to each other on a stone wall, grinning. Not wanting to leave, I stood there thinking of what to do.

From behind the table, a darker-skinned man with a well-kept mustache, slightly turned up on its corners, came out from behind the tree. Wearing a fuchsia turban and a tan cloth wrap draped over his upper body, he walked barefoot toward us across the blackened concrete.

He turned and spoke to the meek salesman in front of me then turned to me, telling me the price of the items. As a smile emerged from my face, I was met by his warm, loving eyes and the most magical smile I've ever seen in return. We all laughed, including the couple to the right.

You know the saying, "To 'assume' is to make an ass out of you and me?" Well, I am totally guilty of making assumptions and judgements, especially on that day. I completely judged the people around me by their appearances, assuming by the clothes they wore that they could or could not speak English. Boy, was I wrong!

I am so grateful for the kindness and patience I was met with that day.

We judge each other by the clothes we wear and the way we speak without ever really knowing much about the other person.

Have you ever made assumptions or judgments about other people?

Have you ever been judged by other people?

I have, and it's no fun. It's time we stop and consider our actions and thoughts, myself included, and practice patience, kindness, and compassion with each other.

One of my favorite quotes from Mahatma Gandhi is, "We but mirror the world. All the tendencies present in the outer world are to be found in the world of our body. If we could change ourselves, the tendencies in the world would also change. As a man changes his own nature, so does the attitude of the world change toward him. This is the divine mystery supreme. A wonderful thing it is and the source of our happiness. We need not wait to see what others do."

In order to create change in the world, we must first look at ourselves and create what we desire for the world within ourselves. The world is your future. Are you willing to look inside yourself and create the change you desire to make the world a better place?

False Realities

"Never be ashamed of what you feel. You have the right to feel any emotion that you want, and to do what makes you happy. That's my life motto."
— Devi Lovato

The picture-perfect family yells at each other behind closed doors.

The girl you want to look like is admitted to a hospital for an eating disorder.

The guy that sits next to you in English slept at a homeless shelter last night because his family was evicted from their house.

The star of the football team's dad was arrested for disorderly conduct.

Things may look a certain way on the outside, but not on the inside.

Everyone has their own stuff going on; you never know what it is. Many people are ashamed, embarrassed, or afraid of what people will think or say, so they hide it, looking perfect on the outside, but suffering on the inside.

Issues and problems are here to help us grow.

If you have a lot going on and don't feel like you can handle it, please find a trusted adult, someone who is a good listener to talk to. People want to help. Processing life's difficulties is hard enough on your own, you don't have to do it alone.

I propose creating a new reality: A world in which we are real and don't judge, gossip, or avoid each other, but accept each other as we are, be kind to each other, and support each other in this big thing called life. Be real. Be honest. Talk. Share. Live.

Together, we can do this. A new reality, a new world.

3

Yep! to This & Adiós! to That

Life Values & Life Dreams

"Desire, ask, believe, receive." — Stella Terrill Mann

What's important to you?
Who do you want to be?
What do you want out of life?

Life Values

Below is a list of values. I want you to choose 5-10 that are important to you. Yeah, I know, it's a huge list and it may not be easy, but I know you can do it. If you already have some in mind that aren't on the list, use those.

Which are important to you?

Authenticity	Adventure	Beauty	Compassion	Creativity
Family	Determination	Faith	Fun	Friendship
Honesty	Responsibility	Justice	Kindness	Knowledge
Leadership	Loyalty	Love	Openness	Optimism
Peace	Recognition	Respect	Humor	Safety
Stability	Self-Respect	Fairness	Wealth	Trustworthiness

Maybe start with those to which you are drawn, however many that may be, then try to narrow it down.

Say to yourself, "If I could only have one, which one would that be?" or "If I could choose one but not the other, which one would I choose?" You'll get a feeling, an inkling. You can always change your mind later, but for now, choose 5-10 Life Values that are most important to you right now in your life.

Write your most important Life Values below.

_____

_____

_____

_____

_____

_____

_____

_____

From all of those, now choose your top 3-5 Life Values and list them below:

_____

_____

_____

_____

_____

Life Dreams

Now, decide on 5-10 Life Dreams you have. Some examples are:

- Have a circle of good friends that I can count on
- End world poverty
- Write a book
- Be a famous singer
- Invent a game
- Be the lead scorer on the soccer team
- Go to my dream college
- Choreograph my own dance
- Record songs
- Be accepted into the Art School of my dreams

"If your dreams don't scare you,
they're not big enough." — Beyoncé

Write them in short, simple phrases. The clearer, the better. Keep it positive and don't be afraid to think big. If you don't want pushy people in your life, then turn it around to something like "I want people in my life who care and listen to me." It's short, simple and positive. Another example is, "I want to be a starting soccer player." You can add more specific information, if you'd like, or not. For example, "I want to be a starting soccer player for my dream team," or "I will have 1 million hits on YouTube for my music." Whatever it is, don't be shy. This is not the time to play small.

Write 5-10 Life Dreams below.

_____

_____

_____

_____

_____

_____

_____

_____

Now, ask yourself if you could pick only 3-5, which would they be? If you need to, use the same process as you did for your Life Values to narrow it down.

Don't let your thoughts or someone else's thoughts get in the way of your dreaming. These are YOUR dreams, not your parents' dreams nor anyone else's.

Which would feel awesome right now in your life?

Write your top 3-5 Life Dreams below.

_____

_____

_____

_____

_____

"Go ahead and believe that no one shines brighter than you. Become amazing, and be happy." — Demi Lovato

Warrior Statement

What do you stand for? Who will you be in this world?

Combine your Life Values and your Life Dreams into one statement below, forming your Warrior Statement. For example, "I live with adventure, honesty, and humor everyday, sharing my music with the world, and surrounding myself with fun friends that have my back." Now, it's your turn! Write your personal Warrior Statement below.

_____

_____

_____

_____

In the back of the book, you'll find the "My Life Values & Life Dreams" and "My Warrior Statement" pages. Write them down, tear 'em out and put 'em on your mirror, next to your bed, or somewhere you'll see them on a regular basis.

You can take a picture of it with your phone or create something fun with it. The point is to look at it all the time. It's easy to get caught up with your friends, texting, social media, video games, and everything else. Having your Life Values & Life Dreams in front of you will help to stay focused on what you really want in life. When you have a decision or choice to make, ask if it aligns with them. If yes, you're good to go. If no, you may want to re-think things.

You can use this process with any part of your life.

For example, running a marathon was a Life Dream of mine. In order to run a marathon, I had to train. In order to train, I had to eat well, get a good night sleep, and spend a lot of time running. However, my friends weren't training for a marathon. Every Friday and Saturday night, they'd call me up to go out. I had to ask myself: which was more important to me, training for my marathon or going out with my friends? The marathon was a Life Dream of mine and in order to achieve it, I had to choose training.

It wasn't always easy. I remember choosing to go out with my friends one Friday night and stayed out too late. I had a terrible training run the next day, confirming that training was more important than going out for me at that time. The next time they called during training, I knew my answer.

Your Life Values, Life Dreams, and Warrior Statement will help you stay on track. Looking at them and choosing in favor of them every day will also help de-stress and de-dramatize your life.

You live and learn from the choices you make. Choose what aligns with your Life Values and Life Dreams and your life will be magical.

Don't Just Dream About It

"Happiness is not something ready made. It comes from your own actions." — Dalai Lama

Now that you figured out what's important to you and what you want for yourself, you've got to decide if you want to be and do your dream or just dream about it. Dreamers simply dream. They sit around and talk about what they want, but they don't do anything to achieve them. Be-ers and doers achieve their dreams; they take action steps to make their dreams a reality.

Go to **www.TruePowerTeens.com** to get some free help with this. *The Day Dreamer's Action Plan* will walk you through steps to help you become your dream and not just dream about it.

The Dump

Now it's time for the big dump! I want you to get all your frustration, unfairness, anger, whatever is weighing you down out of you right now. Yep - right here, right now!

You may be hesitant because you've never done it before, you've never been allowed to dump all your frustrations out and say what you really want to say, but I'm giving you permission to do so.

Grab a sheet of paper and write it, draw it, doodle it, scribble it, whatever you gotta do — get it all out! No one's going to read it, it's not going to be graded, it doesn't have to be pretty, just do it.

You may have a lot, you may have a little. If you need more room, grab some extra paper. Get into a place where you have some privacy and give yourself as much time as you think you need and go for it!

What frustrates you, bums you out, gets you angry, makes you want to stay in bed all day, and completely gets you down? Just spit it out onto the paper. Write it, draw it, doodle it, scribble it, whatever you gotta do — get it all out - right here, right now!

Now, without reading it, go back and just glaze your eyes over that massive amount of stuff that just weighs you down and gets in the way of you living a life that you want for yourself. If you focus on all that, your life will totally bum you and everyone around you out.

Nobody wants that — not even you - so tear it up. Yep! You do not need it any longer. Your life is about to change and you can say "Adios" to all that.

Crumple it up, tear it into small pieces, wet it, throw it into the garbage, light it on fire (think safety, please), walk to the corner and put it into the trash can there, whatever you gotta do — get rid of it!

This is your life, not your mother's, not your father's, not your brother's, sister's, not your friend's, but yours and yours alone. It's your turn to step up and take the True Power that is yours and live the life you deserve.

There are moments throughout your life that have shaped who you are. You gather memories, experiences, and then you create thoughts and beliefs around them to form who you are right now. What you may or may not know is that it's all made up. It's the story you're living. You created it and if you don't like parts of it, you can change them.

Many people think their life is set in stone: what happens, happens, and life is always going to be that way. But it's not and you have the power, your True Power, to change it. There is fear and there is love. Love will lead you to True Power, but only if you choose it.

By the end of this book, it is my hope that you'll know how to access your True Power, your life force, and have a life full of freedom — to be you, one-hundred-percent.

4
Giving Up & Giving In

Stress Stinks

"Doing something that is productive is a great way to alleviate emotional stress. Get your mind doing something that is productive." — Ziggy Marley

KELSEY

The smell of coffee lingered in the long-darkened room. Kelsey, a sophomore, sat in front of me, hunched over. Her light brown hair draped across her forehead and hung down to her shoulders. Her eyes gazed downward toward the dusty floor.

Sitting only two feet apart, I felt the miles of space between us.

Men and women of various ages surrounded us, slouching over their laptops at tables nearby with empty coffee cups and espresso glasses next to them. Fingertips tapped vigorously as they stared at the screens opposite them.

I asked Kelsey why we were meeting.

Her head lifted slightly as her eyes raised to meet mine. Tears broke free from their tight hold, dripping one by one down her delicate face onto the table below. Mumbling streamed out of her petite mouth. Her body collapsed into the fold of her chair.

I couldn't understand every word she said, but I got the message.

Stress.

Kelsey was behind in school. She'd gotten behind before, in middle school and freshman year, but never like this. There were only two weeks before grades came out and she didn't know what to do. She'd always been the "A" student, the smart kid in class with all the answers but now she wasn't and she didn't know how to deal with it.

JOSH

The sun peeked its way through the puffy white clouds as Josh drove home from school. He felt the warmth inside the car even though there were remnants of snow still on strips of grass next to the road. When he got home, he pranced up to the front door, knowing no one would be home for a while.

He dropped his bag on the floor just inside the front door and crashed on the couch, decompressing.

Sucked into the TV show he was watching, he didn't even hear his mom come home. From the kitchen, she yelled, "Did you talk to your teachers yet? You still haven't gotten in your missing work."

His mom griped to him every day, asking when he was going to get his missing work done. Giving in, he flipped the TV off and dragged himself up to his room, grabbing his bag on the way.

Shutting the door behind himself, he dropped his bag on the floor and plopped down onto his bed. A heavy sigh spewed from his lungs.

Day after day, he sat in his room, looking at his books. He did the homework he had for that day, hoping that was good enough, but knowing it wasn't. His mom tried to help but that didn't work; they just ended up screaming at each other.

Josh tried to ignore the fact that there was a problem. He knew he had missed classes, that he was behind, but he didn't know what to do about it. He simply didn't know how to catch up.

RACHEL

Staring at the ceiling, Rachel lay flat as a board on her bed. Her red and blue plaid shirt and black leggings covered her tense torso and limbs. She reached over and grabbed her phone and put her headphones on to block out the bickering back and forth coming from the kitchen. She lay there, dozing in and out, for hours until her mom came to get her to eat dinner.

Rachel didn't even realize she was stressed out until she started to talk about it. She hated being home and tried to be out as much as she could. She had a hard time focusing at school and hardly ever knew what was going on in class.

"Many teens report feeling overwhelmed and depressed or sad as a result of stress. More than one-third of teens report fatigue or feeling tired and nearly one-quarter of teens report skipping a meal due to stress[4]."

Stress looks different for everyone but affects everyone the same way. It brings you down and holds you back from moving forward with your life.

How is stress affecting you? How do you handle it?

---

[4] http://www.apa.org/news/press/releases/2014/02/teen-stress.aspx

In a couple pages, I share some ways to lessen stress; maybe you have more to add to the list. If so, please share. We're all in this together — to help each other through life!

Mind Games

"Don't you ever let a soul in the world tell you that you can't be exactly who you are." — Lady Gaga

I kindly shook both of their hands as I nodded, "Nice to meet you." Just as I heard their frustration on the phone, I could read it on their faces and in their bodies, too. Eleven years of this had gotten old, and they were tired of it.

They introduced me to their son, Andrew, then walked to the other side of the cafe, leaving Andrew and I to get acquainted. All I knew about Andrew was that he was failing most of his classes, he wouldn't do his homework and if he did, he'd forget to hand it in. His parents, divorced, nagged on him every day about it. He was sixteen years old and they'd been dealing with this since elementary school.

In their opinion, Andrew simply didn't care.

Andrew and I sat across from each other at a square table. His chair was pushed back, creating more space between us. His right elbow rested on the table, his back slouched over almost parallel to the floor. His head looked down most of the time except when he spoke, then he'd raise his eyes, but not his head. Andrew's response to most of my questions was, "I don't know."

It felt like we had the whole place to ourselves. There was a stillness in the air, a bubble-like formation around us, leaving all others in the cafe far away from the two of us. As we spoke, I sensed the deep wounds of "I'm not worthy" and self-hatred inside Andrew. He knew everyone had lost hope in him.

Questions and responses were filtered with moments of silence. I sat patiently, feeling the pain and discomfort he was having.

Finally, after gathering some insight around Andrew and what was going on, I realized something, something his parents hadn't mentioned to me before. I paused for a moment, digesting my revelation, then shared it with him.

"You're super smart, aren't you?" I asked.

His head lifted and our eyes met straight on.

I continued, "That's it. You're super smart, and you're bored." He just looked at me.

"Am I right?" I asked again.

He nodded yes.

In the weeks that followed, I got to know more about Andrew and how he became the kid who was failing the majority of his classes and seemed not to care about his life any longer. In kindergarten, he learned that he wasn't good enough because he didn't read as fast as others. In first grade, his friend laughed at him and told him that he couldn't be the astronaut he wished to be.

By fourth grade, he'd attended so many parent/teacher conferences and meetings, hearing over and over about how he wasn't working to his potential, he simply had given up and his parents and teachers began to do the same. Andrew built up a wall of self-sabotaging beliefs (a.k.a. self put-downs) in his head, forgetting who he was and all the good he had to offer the world.

Our minds can be quite the tricksters, just like Andrew's, stopping us from moving forward and believing in ourselves.

Ever ask yourself why you are the way you are? Like why you believe certain things and not others or why you act a certain way around some people and not others? It's no coincidence. You were born an innocent baby and from then you've learned everything you know today, from the way you act to the thoughts and beliefs you have each and every day. It's all been learned.

Some things you intentionally learn, like how to ride a bike. When you set out to learn to ride a bike, you either think you can or think you can't. But, usually, you make it happen and your thoughts turn into a strong belief that you can, because you did.

With other beliefs, you may not even know you have them or how you got them. For example, you may have the belief that you're not good at math or maybe it's drawing or talking to people, or whatever it is - you believe you can't do it.

You may even come from a family that is not good at it, either. Who are you to be any different from anyone else in your family? Your thoughts built up a wall, limiting yourself to what you can and cannot do in this world.

But, what I now know and want you to know, is that it's all learned and you can unlearn it, if you want to.

What if you decided to conquer whatever it is you say you can't do, maybe math or speaking in front of others, with the same determination as learning to ride a bike?

What if you said to yourself, "If other people can do it, I can, too." What if you gave up the belief that's blocking you from learning and lived in the "What if" world of thinking instead?

Cross over to a world of hope, of open choices, fun, and confidence. It's a much more liberating world than the blocked, limited one so many people live in. The choice is yours. You can create new beliefs for yourself anytime you want. Just try it!

For every belief you have, ask:

- Is it aligned with my Life Dreams and Life Values?
- Is it true?
- Is it mine? (Or, did I learn it from someone else?)
- Do I want to keep it or let it go?

Addictions as Coping Mechanisms

"So wake me up when it's all over, When I'm wiser and I'm older, All this time I was finding myself, and I didn't know I was lost."
— Avicii, *Wake Me Up* song lyrics

My eyes opened to the bright stream of light beaming through the sheer curtained window. I stared up at the tall cream-colored ceiling, my body numb and stiff. My tongue, void of any moisture, felt thick and crusty.

"How did I get here?" I asked myself as my eyes searched the room for clues.

I lifted the covers; glancing below, I realized I still had on the clothes I wore the night before. I lowered the covers and closed my eyes, trying to recall the happenings of the night. Nothing but pain shot through my head, front to back. My eyes squinted in agony. The last thing I remembered was being in the bathroom of the teen club.

It was Saturday of Memorial Day weekend. The sky still bright, I ventured out with three friends in celebration of my sixteenth birthday. "Teen Night" was the ultimate destination but not before we got liquored up. Already heavily intoxicated from drinking cheap 18% ABV (alcohol by volume) wine, we downed a couple swigs of tequila and made our way out the door, swaying down the outdoor stair well, one step at a time.

Sarah's mom picked us up at the corner. Squeezing into the backseat, we laughed and sang our way to the club. The 3.5-mile trip only took us ten minutes. Her mom pulled into the parking lot. We each got out of the car and strolled to the front door, money already in hand.

That's all I remember. I was home in bed by eight while two of my friends were at the local hospital having their stomachs pumped.

You hear it all the time, "We're just having fun. Everyone's doing it." But my friends and I are lucky to be alive. Alcohol poisoning and binge drinking are no joke.

"On average, alcohol is a factor in the deaths of 4,358 young people under age 21 each year[5]."

"Research indicates that alcohol use during the teenage years could interfere with normal adolescent brain development and increase the risk of developing an AUD (alcohol use disorder). In addition, underage drinking contributes to a range of acute consequences, including injuries, sexual assaults, and even deaths — including those from car crashes[6]."

We all know this stuff, we learn it in health class. We just don't think it applies to us.

All addictions, whether it's social media, alcohol, drugs, or something else, are a form of escapism, escaping from yourself or from your life, in hopes of finding some sort of self-happiness. Many people, like myself, used alcohol and drugs to fit in. They all are temporary fixes that only take us deeper into whatever pain we've got going on in life.

But there are a lot of young people who choose not to do drugs or drink alcohol. They are having fun being themselves, not being sucked into peer pressure but instead, using their time to accomplish great things. They are working toward their Life Dreams, making a difference in the world, and feeling good. Drugs and alcohol are a

---

[5] https://pubs.niaaa.nih.gov/publications/UnderageDrinking/
Underage_Fact.pdf
[6] https://pubs.niaaa.nih.gov/publications/UnderageDrinking/
Underage_Fact.pdf

distraction and can lead you down a path away from your life purpose.

How do you choose to live your life?

"You have brains in your head. You have feet in your shoes. You can steer yourself any direction you choose."
— Dr. Seuss

5

Build Your Strength

Soup-Can Strength

"The way to get started is to quit talking and begin doing." — Walt Disney

Smelling the fresh spring air, I walked on the light green-colored wooden planks, noticing the two white flower boxes hanging from the railing to my left, full of artificial pink and red geraniums. At the end, I pulled the screen door toward me and held it open with my foot.

Leaning slightly against the mahogany door, I glanced through the thick glass window and reached below for the bronze doorknob. My grandma sat, peering through her magnifying glass, reading the newspaper at the dining room table. The corners of my mouth turned up as my gaze softened.

I turned the knob and pushed the heavy door across the brown marbled carpet. Her eyes looked up, not moving her head or magnifying glass-held hand yet; she smiled. She delicately placed the magnifying glass down, raised her torso, sat back against the wooden chair, and welcomed me with a grin.

My grandma's house was my second home. I spent many Friday and Saturday nights as a child watching The Love Boat and Fantasy Island with her. As she and I grew older, we rented movies and watched them together, eating popcorn and strawberry ice cream. She'd lose her long-lived self in the wonderment of The Lord of the Rings and laugh at the silliness of There's Something About Mary.

Opposite the front door, past the dining room, a tall, wide square archway opened up to the pale yellow and brown printed linoleum tiled kitchen. Sunlight gleamed across the room, exposing dust particles in the air. Aunt Jemima, the prized possession of the house, resided on the countertop, usually full of homemade chocolate chip, oatmeal raisin, or peanut butter cookies.

I shut the door behind me, smelling something delicious in the air. I laid my light jacket on the chair inside the door and made my way to the refrigerator. Opening it, she told me there's green bean casserole if I want any. "Maybe later," I replied as I closed the refrigerator door and made my way to the back of the kitchen.

I lifted the lid of Aunt Jemima and peered inside. Just as I thought, freshly made chocolate chip cookies! I reached my right hand in, feeling around, and grabbed two. With cookies in hand, I made my way back to the dining room table and sat in the wooden chair adjacent to my gram.

Gram had gray and white short hair and wore gold-rimmed glasses. She had a natural pink tone to her cheeks, and I smelled the remnants of Oil of Olay on her fair skin.

Eating one cookie at a time, I told her about my day. She then told me about her latest projects of wanting to repaint the railing on the front porch and organize the boxed photos upstairs. Stopping mid-sentence, she held up her right index finger, and told me to wait there.

Shoulders hunched over, she turned and walked out to the kitchen, left foot then right, stabilized with her taupe Annie Lo shoes bought at the local JC Penney store. Her apron, tied in the back, hung down from her broad waist.

I sat waiting. A minute or two later, she came back from around the corner, with two soup cans in hand. Her long frail fingers, etched with purple veins, housed one lone silver ring with diamonds on her left ring finger. She placed the cans on the table in front of me.

My eyebrows rose as my eyes widened in question. Using her right hand on the table, she slowly lowered herself back down to the chair. She leaned back, taking a minute to rest.

Then, sitting up, she pushed one soup can toward me and pulled one toward her. Lowering her chin, she looked at me, and stated, "My doctor says I need to keep my strength up and you're going to help me."

I thought she was kidding.

Just as I started to smirk, she took one can in her right hand, turned it to the right, palm facing up, and brought it to the side of the table. I quickly realized this was no joke. Lowering it, she rested it on the inside of her violet polyester pants and signaled for me to begin.

Gram bent her elbow up, lifting the can to her shoulder then lowered it again. She looked at me and nodded to follow. I grabbed the remaining soup can, lowered it down, and pulled it back up to my shoulder, just like her. We sat there counting to ten, doing soup-can arm curls together.

My gram was 90 years old. She could have easily blown off what her doctor said and watched TV instead. But she didn't. She chose to do what it took to keep her strength up, to love herself, and to improve her life.

So many people want their life to be better, to be different from what it is, but they sit around doing nothing, waiting for it to happen or for someone to do it for them. We all have a choice; we can sit around and wait for things to change or we can start taking action.

"If you want to be the best, you have to do things that other people aren't willing to do."
— Michael Phelps

My gram didn't start by lifting a fifty-pound barbell, she lifted a ten-ounce can of soup, one arm at a time. She built her strength up and didn't give in to what other people said or thought. Instead, she did what it took to make it happen and she got me to help her. Start with what you have, learn from others, get good teachers, have a support system, and go for it!

The Soup-Can Strength Mantra:
"I matter. My choices matter.
No matter what, the world needs me."

De-Stress Yourself

"When everything in life gets so complicated, it only takes a day to change it." — Bruno Mars

It's no secret that stress is a silent killer. School, your little brother, friends, teachers, the soccer game, your parents, the future, the past, final exams, the world, anything, can cause stress in your life — if you let them.

Stress is living in fear, it's when you get into survival mode. It can make you sick, wear down your immune system, and block your brain from functioning correctly. It's a huge power depleter!

Maybe you live in a toxic area, with emotional, physical, or mental abuse occurring in your house, like Rachel. That can be extremely stressful. Avoidance and procrastination, like Kelsey and Josh, can cause stress, too. Even the incessant "I don't know" like Andrew can spiral you out of control, not even realizing how much stress you're causing yourself.

Stress makes life more difficult to handle. It's hard to function at 100% when your body is under so much stress. Sleep deprivation, living off sugar and caffeine, and eating unhealthy foods all put stress on your body, too.

What's the cause of your stress?

Ways to Lessen the Stress:

- Change your environment to help change what your mind is fixating on
- Laugh it off
- Watch or listen to something funny
- Do something you enjoy
- When you're overwhelmed, decide one small thing you can do to help yourself
- Get lots of sleep
- Exercise
- Eat well
- Go outside and get fresh air
- Sit, breathe, let things go
- Give yourself alone time (with no technology)

My mind is the cause of my stress everyday—I create it! It goes crazy by telling, re-telling, and obsessing over things. You name it, my mind can create it – spinning it out of control and creating a ton of stress for myself. Even though I'm your guide through all of this, I'm still human just like you.

Busy minds (like crazy minds), as opposed to calm minds, create an enormous amount of unneeded stress for many people. Thoughts that continuously repeat in your head and the belief systems that hold you back cause you stress.

Stress is our reaction to what's going on around us. Once we realize that it's not them, the people and things around us, but it's actually ourselves, we can start to create the change that we want. We can begin to let go and start again.

Notice when your mind is going out of control, breathe, figure out your choices, choose, and come back to right now, the present moment.

5 Steps to De-Stress:

1. Stop and notice the stress
2. Breathe
3. Figure out your choices (to let it go or not)
4. Choose
5. Come back to the present moment

If you practice these five steps, you'll begin to notice the results of your choices. By choosing to let it go, your stress level will reduce and you'll be more relaxed. If you don't, you'll continue to feel stressed and exhausted from what's going on around you.

"You have power over your mind — not outside events.
Realize this, and you will find strength."
— Marcus Aurelius

6

Shatter the Struggle

The Stench of Self-Sabotage

"One advantage of talking to yourself is that you know at least somebody's listening."
— Franklin P. Jones

According to the Laboratory of Neuro Imaging at the University of Southern California, "The average person has about 48.6 thoughts per minute. That adds up to a total of 70,000 thoughts per day[7]." I knew my mind was busy, but I never knew it was that busy!

"I'm not good enough" is the world's most used thought and belief that holds people back. I'm sure if you cracked open all the minds around you and looked inside of them, you would see a few "I'm not good enough" thoughts, if not a ton more.

The thought, "I'm not good enough," is rampant and hugely disastrous. If that thought rules your mind, you have a choice: to let it go and move forward or give up and let it rule you.

The people who choose to give up and let it rule them never move forward in life. They get stuck. They let their thoughts rule their lives in a negative, limiting way. They are the ones who sit around and wait for life to happen.

Some blame everyone else for the life they don't have and compare themselves to others, always thinking they can't be what they want to be, while others choose to let

---

[7] https://www.reference.com/world-view/many-thoughts-per-minute-cb7fcf22ebbf8466#

those limiting thoughts go and move forward, evolving and being successful no matter what. They start being what they want to be no matter what others say or do. They put aside limiting thoughts that may come in and move toward what they want for themselves and their life.

Comparing yourself to others, worrying about what others think or say, and self-put-downs are all forms of self-sabotage.

"I'm not good enough" and all thoughts that mimic it like, "I can't do that," "I'm not smart enough," "They are better than I am," or "I don't have what they have," all need to be put aside. Beliefs like these get in the way of you being you and living your life the way you would like to. They are like a big, fat, red stop sign in front of you, keeping you from having the life you want and deserve.

What if you just pushed delete from your interior mind playlist? What if you never had another thought that put you down and got in your way? Wouldn't that be awesome? Then you could make your own personal playlist with all the good stuff, your own True Power Playlist (TPP), with thoughts such as "I am good enough," "I'm smart," "I'm awesome," "My hair rocks," and all the other great stuff you already know about yourself.

Your mind believes what you tell it until it's proven right or wrong. Just like I said earlier, before you succeeded at riding a bike, you may have said "I can't" in your head, but those thoughts changed to "I can" soon after you did it, proving your mind wrong. The moment your mind believes it's possible, it changes from "I can't" to "I can." Then you're off, riding your bike, and living confidently in the world.

Before you move on to the next chapter, take time to write down a True Power Playlist (TPP) for yourself then read it over and over again. When you're having a moment of self-sabotage, come back to your True Power Playlist. Breathe the words in and let go of anything that's holding you back.

My True Power Playlist (TPP)

_____

_____

_____

_____

_____

_____

_____

_____

_____

*"You can tell a lot about a person
by what's on their playlist."*
— Keira Knightley, movie quote from *Begin Again*

Worrying Wars

"Don't worry when you are not recognized, but strive to be worthy of recognition." — Abraham Lincoln

If you had a choice between peace and happiness or struggle and anxiety, which would you choose? Duh! That's a stupid question, right?! But a lot of people worry about a lot of things.

What do you worry about?

- What to wear
- What people think
- If you fit in
- If it's safe to go home tonight
- If he or she likes you or not
- If you're going to get into college
- Money

Worrying is wanting to know what you don't know. It's like we want to know what's going to happen so we fixate on what could happen which totally drags us down and makes our minds spiral out of control worrying about what could be - but isn't real. It's like we want to control everything but we can't. We want to know what other people are thinking, are saying, and we focus on that. The more we obsess, the more stressed-out we get.

I have a friend who seems to worry a lot. She's always preoccupied with what others are going to say or think. It can be pretty exhausting to be around her. Although I totally know that worrying is a complete drag, I still can get caught up in it. I've had plenty of times when I worry about the future and want to know what it is going to happen. But I can't.

What about you? Do you worry about things a lot or have people in your life who do?

Like everything else, there's a hidden benefit to worrying. For me, worrying about the future helps me avoid what I need to do right now. It's a distraction. It keeps me safe from change. And, it's completely driven by fear and my ego mind.

The mind can be pretty manipulative. We make up stories all the time, stopping us from thinking and knowing that we can be and do what we want to in life. It's like when Andrew gave up on his dream to be an astronaut just because a couple people made comments about it and he believed them. He began to tell himself that he couldn't do it.

If we let fear and worry consume us, then we stay in our safe place, not acting on our dreams and desires, but instead moping around wishing it were different. This repeats over and over until we realize we can change it. That's the True Power we all have inside of us.

When you let go of worry and fear, then you relax and things start to happen, moving you forward toward your dreams.

Have you ever been so worried about something you can't get it off your mind? It's like an octopus has taken over your mind and its pink, suction-cup tentacles are flying every which way, reaching for answers that you need right now. Then, in the midst of a thought, something or someone gets your attention and your obsessed mind releases for a moment. The distraction of something or someone else frees your mind. Your body lets go of the tight hold of thoughts, and maybe, just maybe, you're open enough to get a glimpse of what you need in that moment, the answer, solution, or idea that you were searching for.

When you can let go of the worry or obsessive thoughts, the answers arrive.

For example: If you're thinking, "What if I don't get into the class I want?" You can simply say to yourself, "It's all good. If I get in, awesome; if I don't, I'll figure something else out." Don't wait around worrying, you'll know when you know. Until then, do something you enjoy.

Here's another example: Switch your thinking from, "What if he says, 'No'?" to "What if he says 'Yes'?" Thinking the first one with 'no' causes a sense of hopelessness. Thinking with 'yes' causes a sense of hope and excitement.

Going down the negative spiral of worry, fear, and doubt, will totally make you crazy. Or, you can do the opposite and let it go, move forward, and focus on the possibilities.

A Different Perspective

"We cannot change the cards that we are dealt, just how we play the hand." — Unknown

What if everything that has happened in your life was meant to happen?

What if what you see as "bad" is actually "good" in some way?

What if you asked yourself: How can this be fun? How can this get better? Instead of telling yourself how much you hate something or how bad it is?

What would it be like if you changed your perspective on situations, people, and events in your life? How would your life change for the better?

Reap the Benefits of Responsibility

"I'm one with the Force. The Force is with me."
— Chirrut Îmwe, *Rogue One: A Star Wars Story*

EMMA

I sat across from the computer screen, listening to Emma's never-ending complaints about her teacher and school. Emma was about 5'6" tall with long dark hair and deep brown eyes. Concert posters lined the bedroom wall behind her. As she spoke, her hands moved back and forth in the air.

Her mother contacted me because Emma had complained about herself, school, and lack of friends for so long that she needed someone outside of herself to help.

Sitting patiently, I felt the aggravation, unfairness, and deep hurt she had inside.

Emma had been diagnosed with dyslexia years ago and school had never been easy for her. She had an IEP (Individualized Education Program) and was given more time on homework and tests. She'd gone through years of being different, being bullied, and being unhappy. Today was no different.

Frustrated, she complained that her science teacher wasn't following her IEP and giving her the extra time she was allotted for the assignment that was due on Friday. She complained to her mom, she complained to me, and she probably complained to her friends, too.

Nobody else had to do what she had to do. No one else had to have their mom talk to the teacher time and time again about the guidelines of her IEP and to remind them that, by law, they needed to follow those guidelines. It had gotten old and Emma was tired of dealing with it every year, especially with all the other high-school stuff that was going on.

I let her get it all out.

After several minutes, I took my turn.

I asked her one simple question, "Did you speak to the teacher about this?"

Her answer to this question went on and on. The short answer was no. She had told her mom about it, me, and her friends, but never the teacher, the source of her problem, and the one person responsible for the solution.

"Would you be willing to speak directly to your teacher about this?" I asked.

I watched as her body relaxed and her eyes turned downward.

She agreed.

The next fifteen minutes were spent brainstorming on how to have a respectful conversation with her teacher so she could walk away getting what she wanted and feeling good about the situation.

The next day, Emma used her True Power to solve her own problem. She waited until all the other students had left class then she walked up to her teacher. In a respectful, calm manner, she told the teacher exactly what she wanted and asked for what she needed. Her teacher was very receptive. She got the time she was allowed and walked away feeling successful and proud of herself.

ANA

School was the last place Ana wanted to be. She had hated it since the seventh grade, when her "friends" decided to not like her anymore. Ana was a freshman and she truly thought things would be different now that she was at a different school with more people. But she was wrong, the same kind of stuff was happening in high school that happened in middle school.

Ana was medium height, with dirty blonde hair, and wore round, black-rimmed glasses. When I asked if she wanted to change schools, do home school, online school, or some other alternative, she always said no. She preferred to complain and blame others rather than to do anything about it.

She had a choice.

As much as she wanted to be done with school, she also knew she had to finish in order to move on with her life. She didn't want to quit and, deep down, she wanted to like school. She wanted school to be fun.

After Ana realized that the choice was hers to make and she'd be fully supported in that decision, she chose to stay at the same school. However, she had to change the way she was being in order to change the experience she was having. She had to stop complaining and focusing on everything she didn't like and start looking at the good stuff.

Instead of always putting other people down in her head, she had to lower her guard and begin to treat other people more kindly. She decided to join a club that she never would have done previously. She started to meet new people and make new friends.

By senior year, she was happy she had stayed at her school. Her life changed because she took responsibility for her happiness and changed the way she was being.

Life happens no matter what but by taking responsibility for your happiness, things can change for the better. All you have to do is decide to change; then go from there.

Avoidance

"The battles that count aren't the ones for gold metals. The struggles within yourself — the invisible, the inevitable battles inside all of us — that's where it's at." — Jesse Owens

I don't know about you, but there have been many times I wanted to avoid life at all costs; to run away, start over, and live someone else's life. We've already talked about how people use drugs and alcohol to escape from reality; some people use video games, books, food, the internet, social media, and TV, too.

Avoidance doesn't make anything go away, it just prolongs the pain. I've avoided plenty in my life and I still catch myself doing it. It's like when you procrastinate on doing your homework or talking to your parent, friend, boss, or teacher about something. You don't want to do it, so you don't. You wait it out. But at the same time, your mind thinks about it all the time so you're really not free from the situation until you do whatever it is you're trying to avoid. I've done this many times in my life.

What I finally figured out is the sooner I can just get it done and take whatever action steps I need to take, then I can move on without any lingering thoughts going around and around in my head. I can actually just hang out and know it's taken care of. You get it?

Alcohol, drugs, and avoiding responsibility didn't work for me, but digging deep within myself and doing my own self-work did. There will be moments in your life that you think things will never get better, but they will. It does take time. It does take responsibility. And, it does take self-love, but it's worth it and you are worth it. Keep going. Have faith. You got this!

I Don't Know, Do You?

"Live your life with arms wide open. Today is where your book begins. The rest is still unwritten."
— Singer, songwriter Natasha Bedingfield

Just like Andrew, "I don't know" was my answer to everything. It drove my parents up the wall. It was sort of my way of tuning out and really not caring. I've worked with several young people and "I don't know" is a common term used by many!

But I figured out why I didn't know all the time. It was because I learned to not know, just like you've learned to not know, too. I've watched it play out so many times.

When you were young, you did know and you actually knew all the time. You knew the answers, you knew what you wanted from the menu at a restaurant, and you knew what you wanted in life, but it may not have been the acceptable answer for the adults around you, so you learned to not know and "I don't know" became the forever answer to everything.

Adults were the ones who answered for you and didn't allow you to access your True Power, to nurture it and cultivate it to use for the rest of your life. Over time, you let their answer be yours and little by little, you lost touch with your True Power, your inner guidance system, and your own answers. You let it go, realizing it was easier to let others make the decisions for you than having to deal with them.

Then all of a sudden, the adults around you that warped you into this "I don't know" person that you became, got frustrated at you for not having an answer and not knowing. They didn't even realize they were the ones who taught you to not know.

But it's up to you to get back in touch with YOU and your True Power source and start gaining your inner knowing back.

You know what you want and you know what you don't want. You know what's good for you and you know what's not. Start making choices and decisions that align with your Life Values; that will get you closer to your Life Dreams and bring you Life Joy.

The sooner you speak up for yourself and let your knowing come through, the sooner you will be on your way to great things.

"The first step towards getting somewhere is to decide that you are not going to stay where you are."
— Unknown

7

Choose Wisely

Choices Matter

"May the force be with you." — Obi-Wan Kenobi,
Star Wars: Episode III - Revenge of the Sith

No, you're not crazy, but you definitely talk to yourself, just as everyone else does. We have two voices in our mind leading and questioning our every move. There's the voice that criticizes you and there's the voice that praises you. You may have parents who do the same thing, but the voices I'm talking about right now are the voices in your head doing it to you.

One voice comes from your True Power, which is sourced from your heart; it's that gut feeling, an instinct or inkling you get. It's your true knowing. It helps you live life in alignment with your values. Choices made from that True Power source always feel good. True Power is in us all; it fills our hearts and souls.

The other voice, on the other hand, creates a lot of confusion and leads you down a different path, a path away from your heart, your values, and your life dreams. That voice is sourced from your ego mind and it can be an easy distraction from happiness and self-love.

If you make choices that align with your Life Values and Life Dreams, they will get you closer to the peace and freedom you're looking for. If you think too much and go back and forth on your decisions, then it could be the ego mind, the other voice in your head, causing a distraction, and leading you away from your Life Dreams.

Your choices either fuel your energy or suck it out of you.

"It is our choices, Harry, that show what we truly are,
far more than our abilities."
— Dumbledore, *Harry Potter and the Chamber of Secrets*
by J.K. Rowling

How do you choose to spend your time?
Is it helping you get closer to your Life Dreams or taking
you farther away from them?
What music do you choose to listen to?
Are the lyrics positive or negative?
Does the music make you feel good or
does it make you feel worse?

All of this affects who you are, your mood,
and how you feel.

Who do you choose to hang out with?
Do they uplift you or bring you down?
Do you like hanging out with them or not really?

Make life easy, choose to hang out with people who you
like and who like you.

What choices do you make about money?
Are you saving it or spending it?
Why are you spending or saving your money?

What words are you choosing to use with
yourself and others?
Are they kind or hurtful?

What foods are you choosing to put in your body?
Do they give you energy or are they setting
you up to crash?

Think of what you really want and make choices that match that. If you want energy, eat healthy foods. If you want to feel good and have fun, then hang out with people that like the real you. If you want a car, then start saving your money. If you want the world to be a better place, then be kind to yourself and others.

It's all about choices and it's your choice to make. Say, "Yes, please," to yourself, your Life Values, and your Life Dreams and, "No, thank you," to distractions and doubt.

Honesty is the Best Policy

"Integrity is telling myself the truth. And honesty is telling the truth to other people."
— author Spencer Johnson

Grace was a junior in high school and played in the band. The Monday before a special Saturday performance, she decided she didn't want to play in it. She told her mom and her mom said she didn't have to if she didn't want to.

Grace went to school the next day and told her band teacher she couldn't play at Saturday's event.

Her teacher replied by telling her it would be reflected in her grade if she missed the event. Grace was furious. She went home, told her mother what happened, and her mother immediately called the teacher.

Her mother said they had a family obligation and demanded that the teacher excuse her from the event without lowering her grade. The band teacher responded just as he did with Grace, restating that Grace had signed the syllabus at the beginning of the year and committed to all band events, including the one on Saturday.

Her mother was furious and called the administrator to complain. As a result, Grace didn't play in Saturday's event and her grade was not compromised.

Was that honest? Was it worth it? Did all people involved act with integrity?

How important are honesty and integrity to you?

Adults aren't always the best role models, but that doesn't mean you can't be. The world needs you 100%; don't compromise yourself or your values for others.

High Standards

"Never apologize for having high standards. People who really want to be in your life will rise up to meet them." — Author unknown

We all deserve the best, but some people don't believe it because they haven't ever experienced it. Some lower their standards for others just to fit in, to get someone to like them, or to make others feel comfortable. We all want to be accepted and liked for who we are, but it's not worth lowering your standards to be.

Do you have high standards for yourself or do you lower them for others? Can you be you without compromising your values?

A 17-year-old client of mine told me about this guy she was hanging out with. He wasn't everything she wanted, but she wanted to hang with him nonetheless and see what would happen. He called her all the time to hang out and they texted back and forth. She had fun with him and thought they had fun together, but she still wasn't completely sure about him.

They hung out a few times, then after about three weeks, he started blowing her off in front of his friends. He started to not return her texts, but then would call to hang out on the weekends. It got weird.

The signs were there and she knew she wasn't being treated well. Unfortunately, she was willing to lower her standards to continue to hang out with him when she could. She even started to act the way she thought he wanted her to act. But nothing worked. Nothing changed.

She sat on her bed every day waiting for a text from him. Her heart hurt. She didn't even really like him that much but she wanted him to like her. She felt empty inside and her friends didn't get it. They got tired of her moping around, always talking about him, and wondering what he was doing.

After a couple weeks, her friends got sick of it and told her she had to move on. She didn't want to, but she knew she had to.

Love hurts; not being accepted or liked. But being treated poorly hurts so much more. If you don't believe you deserve the best, no one else will either. Finding that special someone isn't always easy, but having high standards for yourself helps.

Don't give up just because it didn't work with one person. Trust and listen to your heart and it will lead the way for you. No matter what, continue to have high standards for yourself.

"When you set standards and stick to them, there will be people in your life who will fall away. Let them."
— Author Unknown

Chocolate Chip Cookies

"You just gotta keep it happy and keep the vibes going." — song lyrics, from A Tribe Called Quest

The hot chocolate oozed as I took my first bite, crumbs fell to the ground. I wiped the remains from the corners of my lips and licked my fingers making sure to get it all. I loved my grandma's chocolate chip cookies!

We both wore white cotton aprons tied around our waists with smears of food residue on the front from past baking sprees. Standing next to each other in the middle of the kitchen counter, I read the ingredients aloud off the recipe card, soiled from years of use.

"Baking soda," I called. Turning to the right, she reached up and opened the two white cupboard doors above the black microwave oven. Eyeing through all the glass and boxed goods, she grasped the small golden box and placed it on the counter in front of us. Leaving the cupboard doors open, she waited for the next ingredient.

"Vanilla," I called. She turned again to the right and grabbed the small, dark bottle, setting it next to the baking soda. Between the two of us, we soon had all needed ingredients lined up in front of us.

Murphy, her thin Blue Merle Australian Shepherd, barked briefly in the backyard. I stepped up on my tippy toes and peered out the square window, watching him run around in circles. Gram reached in front of me and rasped her knuckles against the glass, stopping Murphy's bark and inviting him back into the house through the doggy door.

With the silver bowl in front of me, Gram handed me the ingredients one by one as the recipe called. As I measured and dumped them into the bowl, she asked me about my life, my work as a lifeguard at the local state park, and my friends. I rattled on about the fun and frustration I was having.

I grabbed the two beaters and inserted them into the Sunbeam Mixmaster until I felt a click. Pausing the conversation, I turned on the mixer and blended the shortening, butter, sugar, eggs, and vanilla together. Once it became a creamy granular texture, I turned it off and continued the conversation. She smiled and laughed at my stories.

I added the flour, baking soda, and salt. Turning the mixer on once more, the conversation paused yet again. As the dough began to take form, the mixer's motor dragged like your history class lecture on a Friday afternoon. I lifted the mixer slowly, letting the dough fly around the interior edge of the bowl until a thin coating of cream colored batter was remaining on the beaters. After turning it off, I un-clicked the beaters and set them on a small white plate back against the wall to savor later.

Leaning against the gold-speckled white counter, my gram told me about her week.

Finally, I poured a cup of semi-sweet chocolate chips into the bowl, making a big heap of brown love in the middle. Picking a couple chips from the top, I plopped them in my mouth and glanced down at Gram. She shook her head from left to right, lowering her lightly powdered face, as her eyes looked up at me and smiled. The chocolate softened on my tongue.

Making cookies with my gram is one of my favorite pastimes. She taught me the value of helping others, listening, and spending quality time with others. I felt heard when I was with her. She was the one constant in my life. She was interested in my life and I loved that about her.

Who is your constant, the person who takes time to listen and support you, and shares life stories with you? Who helps you solve your life problems without telling you what to do, that inspires you to be a better person in the world, and teaches you life lessons just by being themselves?

There are many great people in this world just waiting and wanting to be a mentor and make a difference in someone's life. If you don't have one and would like one, seek them out. There are organizations that match up volunteers as mentors; however, you could already have someone around you who would be a good match - maybe a neighbor, a local business person, or teacher.

Look for a person who is kind and patient. Do they listen as much as they talk? Are they interested in you and your life? Are they positive? Do you get a good vibe about them?

Once you feel you've found that special person, you can either ask them directly to be your mentor or simply start spending time with them, creating a relationship. Feel it out. If you're enjoying your time with them being your true self, learning from them, and listening to them as much as they are listening to you, you've found your match.

"Sometimes it only takes one person
who really believes in you." — Lady Gaga

The Art of Good Listening

"Every good conversation starts with good listening." — Anonymous

One of the greatest traits I cherished about my grandma was her listening skills.

Good listeners are a rare breed. People interrupt, ignore you while you're talking, talk over you, and even speak for you. Many people don't even know how to listen and haven't ever experienced the comfort of being listened to.

Listening is a skill that we seldom are taught or even modeled. You probably know or have people in your life who love to talk; they always are talking and never let you say a word. That's like the opposite of listening, it's just talk, talk, talk. There's nothing wrong with talking - actually I'm a huge advocate of talking - however that's not a dialogue.- it's a monologue.

A dialogue is when two people come together to converse, to talk with one another and listen to each other, to feel heard.

I will teach you how to be a good listener, but be forewarned, just because you learn to be a good listener and you give the gift of listening to others, don't expect it in return. I used to get so frustrated because other people weren't listening to me even though I was listening to them. What I've learned is that you just have to let it go, keep being a good listener, and hope they will learn from you at some point.

The gift of listening can literally change the world. When you are listened to, you feel loved, heard, and accepted. The world needs more of that and you can be its teacher.

How to Listen

- Turn off all distractions and give the other person your full attention.
- Step into their shoes. Feel what they are feeling.
- Listen from their point of view. Get what it's like to be them in that moment.
- Just listen.

- Don't come up with solutions, don't wait for your turn to speak, don't spend your time thinking of what you're going to say next, nothing. Just sit and listen.
- Don't stare them down, doze off, think how they're wrong or stupid for thinking or being that way; don't change the subject, or judge, just listen.
- As you listen, use words and gestures such as, "uh-huh" and "hmmm" to let them know that you're still there and interested.
- That's it. It's that simple!

Important Points to Remember:

- Most of the time, people just want to talk; they may just need to get something off their chest, to say it out loud, and work through it.
- They may ask for your opinion. If they do, ask them what their opinion is first. Help them come up with ideas and solutions for themselves rather than just telling them what you think is best.
- It's not important if you agree or not, just listen and be there for them.
- If they are dealing with a serious situation, recommend they talk to a trusted adult. If they don't want to tell an adult, then you be the one to do it. It's not an easy decision to make and your friend may be mad at you, but if it's a serious situation, you need to keep your friend and others safe.

Listening is a gift, free of charge. Try to give it as often as possible!

Listen to You First

"You have every right to a beautiful life."
— Selena Gómez

The most important person to give the gift of listening to is yourself. Every other person is ready and willing to give you their opinion, their answer, their solution, but you need to listen to YOU first. When you listen to others before yourself, you give your power away.

It's not always easy to reject someone's opinion, but the following guidelines can help.

<u>Guidelines For Handling Other People's Opinions:</u>

-   Let others share their opinions, answers, and solutions.
-   Acknowledge their opinion and thank them kindly. For example: "Yeah, that's a good idea. Thanks," or "That might work. I'll think about it. Thanks."
-   Let their comments go and tap into your True Power, your inner guidance system.
-   Ask yourself what's best for you at that time.
-   Listen and be ready to receive an answer. You'll get a feeling or an inkling - that is your answer.

You have all the answers right inside of you. You just have to ask, wait, and listen.

8

Pain & Blame

Popularity Isn't All It's Cracked Up to Be

"The most important thing to remember is that you can wear all the greatest clothes and all the greatest shoes, but you've got to have a good spirit on the inside. That's what really going to make you look like you're ready to rock the world."
— Alicia Keys

Jamie, one of the star basketball players, appeared fine on the outside but when he got home, he sat in his room with thoughts of ending his life. No one ever knew.

Courtney was considered popular in seventh grade, but in eighth grade things changed. She didn't know what she did. No one would tell her. They started texting her mean stuff and giving her looks in the hallways. She hated it. Courtney tried to play it cool at school but when she got home, she broke down in tears. Her mom didn't know what to do. Courtney didn't want to go to school and often left early with a stomach ache.

Michael's dad got laid off. Although he was told everything would be fine, he could tell his parents were worried. They tried to keep everything from him to protect him, but it didn't work.

I wish I could say these things never happen but you know that's not true. It happens all the time.

You never know what's going on with someone, popular or not. People may wear cool clothes and seem to have all the confidence in the world, but life is life and we all have stuff we're going through whether we show it on the outside or not, whether we talk about it or not.

People go through life covering up their inside hurts to "play it cool," not letting anyone know what's really going on. Popular people have a reputation to uphold and this reputation and way of being can be very stressful, just as stressful as being unpopular. We tend to judge each other for who we are, the stereotype that we are perceived to be, but really, we all have a lot in common.

When it comes to losing a friend, parents getting divorced, being broken up with, or any other difficult thing in life, money, popularity, and the clothes you wear really don't matter.

The best thing you can do for another person is to be kind to them no matter what. A kind gesture or word can make a huge difference for a person who may be hurting in some way.

The more we can help each other, the more the world will be a better place to live. Together, we can make it happen.

What small kind gesture can you share with someone today?

Moody Moments

"I wouldn't live with me, believe me. I'm moody."
— comedian Mario Cantone

Do you ever notice when you are in a bad mood, all you want to do is avoid people, go in your cave and not answer to anyone? You just want to be left alone and no one seems to get it? You feel heavy, tired, and don't really want to do anything. Smiling and talking seem like a chore.

But when you are in a good mood, you want to be around people, and you feel light and energetic. Smiling and talking seem natural.

If bad moods tend to rule your life, think of ways to shift it. Will sulking on the couch help? Probably not. Will playing video games or staring at Instagram help? They may distract you, consume your thoughts, and take up your time, but neither one will really help shift your mood. They might make it worse.

Movement of any kind can help shift your mood from bad to good. Add in some music, singing, laughter and you're sure to shift things for yourself. Maybe parkour is your thing, or biking, or rock climbing. Or, maybe it's dancing around your room. Whatever it is, you gotta do it – it gets you out of your stuck place and into living again and being happy.

6 Mood Shifters:

Laughing
Exercise & movement
Fresh Air
Music
Healthy, yummy food
Connecting with a friend

Stuffed Emotions & Trauma

"Holding onto anger is like grasping a hot coal with the intent of throwing it at someone else. You are the one that gets burned." — Buddha

The puffy clouds blanketed the sky above. Abandoned train cars sprawled on the aged tracks to our right, with sporadic trees, bushes, and weeds to our left. My dad, brother and I were on our bikes, riding down the gravel-lined back road, a narrow, slate-colored path full of potholes and small crevices.

Hearing the chain rap as it circled the chain ring, I gleefully pumped my legs up and down while my shoulders moved back and forth, twisting my body. Pink and purple streamers flowed from the white handle grips. I sped up the dwarf-like hill, spotting the shiny steel strip running diagonally in front of me.

As I hit the metal strip, the front tire swept swiftly to the left. My eyes closed tightly, wincing. My arms braced as my body plummeted twenty inches to the ground and I felt my right knee cap hit the four-inch wide steel strip. My cheek laid against the vintage tar road; I opened my eyes, viewing the earth sideways.

Just as I felt a whimper coming up through my chest into my throat, I heard my dad say, "You're not hurt. Get up." My body cringed and I moved forward, pausing for a moment more. I pulled my right foot out from between the pedal and road. Holding in the tears and pain, I glared down at the ground and I picked myself up.

My eyebrows scrunched together like The Grinch. I brushed the dirt off my elbow and leg, then rubbed my pink wounded knee. I jerked up my bike with my right hand and got back on, biting down on the inside of my left lower lip; I pedaled forward.

I locked those tears inside for many years until I learned the world was a safe place. Trauma can be as small as falling off your bike or as big as a losing someone you love. We all experience trauma in some way in our lives. Working through it, letting your feelings and emotions out, and using words to express yourself all help to release the pain.

Life can definitely be hard at times, but processing your emotions will help dilute the pain and suffering. If you are anything like me, you gotta get your emotions out. It's the only way to heal.

If you're having a moment of anger, frustration, or sadness, try the following steps to help process it:

6 Steps to Processing Negative Emotions:

1. Notice it.
2. Name it.
3. Feel it fully. (Let yourself be sad, angry, frustrated - whatever it is.)
4. Let it go and be here now.
5. Breathe
6. Replace with a Feel-Good emotion (peace, joy, happiness)

For example, if you get mad, notice it. Name it by saying to yourself or out loud, "I'm angry." Then, be angry. Allow yourself to feel the emotion of anger without hurting yourself or others. Time will pass and once you let it move around within you, you'll feel it ease up. When you do, let it go. Then, be here now, in the present moment, without the emotion. Relax, replace it with a feel-good emotion, and breathe it in, noticing how you feel.

You can also try the following to help you through a situation:
- Count to ten slowly, taking abdominal breaths in and out
- Take a walk or run
- Sing
- Dance
- Shake your body
- Talk to a person who is a good listener
  - Tell them, "I just need to talk. I need to get it out. I don't need a solution. I just need you to listen. Can you do that for me?"
  - If they respond with a "Yes," you're good to go. Make sure to thank them when you're done.
  - If they respond with a "No," then thank them for their honesty and move on to someone else.

Source of Pain

"You have to believe in yourself when no one else does." — Serena Williams

Love makes the world go round; it's what brings us joy, happiness, and peace. Wanting other people to give you love before you give it to yourself will eventually lead you to frustration and possibly depression.

When you love yourself, you are giving yourself positive comments, positive talk, making choices that align with your values, and stepping into life. We've talked about this before; fear is the opposite of love. When you're putting yourself down and comparing yourself to others, saying "I can't" and "I'm not good enough," then you're living in fear. Fear is the source of all pain.

What's causing the most pain in your life? What would it be like if you gave up your fear?

7 Steps to Ease the Pain:

1. Close your eyes
2. Breathe
3. Relax your body
4. Imagine your pain, suffering, & struggle leaving you—blow it out to the wind or let it soak into the earth
5. Watch it leave your space
6. Breathe it out
7. Feel peace and freedom inside

Drama, Drama, Drama

"All we have to do is decide what we want to do with the time that is given us." — Gandalf the Grey, *Lord of the Rings - The Fellowship of the Ring*

Gossip, rumors, "he said, she said" consumes the world! I've worked with several teenagers the last few years and what brings them down the most is drama. Drama takes up valuable time, energy, and brainpower.

What if you didn't have it? What would life be like if you had absolutely no drama in your life?

Really. Imagine it - no gossip, no rumors, nothing. Could you live like that?

I know some people who would honestly say "no" and I think that's a scary place to be.

There have been many times I've gossiped and talked about others. I didn't have much else to talk about so I talked about other people. I judged others, like I was any better, right?! If anything, I was envious or jealous of them.

Then one day, I decided to give up gossip, just like that. When I did, I had a huge space in my life. It was like I had nothing to do. I started to panic because I didn't have anything to talk about!

After I got used to not gossiping or spreading rumors, I realized I had a lot more time on my hands. It was pretty cool. I took fun classes and met new people, which kept me too busy to think or talk about other people's lives. I got busy doing things I always wanted to do, things I enjoyed, and I started talking about ideas and events in the world instead of other people.

Quitting drama wasn't easy, especially when so many people around me did it. I still get sucked into it from time to time but now I realize what a waste of time it is. Social media can be the same thing, an energy drainer, power depleter, and waste of time.

It's not easy to change, but it's worth it. Give it a try. Try giving up drama (and maybe a little social media, too) and see what that small change can do for you.

Eleanor Roosevelt said, "Great minds discuss ideas. Average minds discuss events. Small minds discuss people." I say, "We need more great minds in this world — stop the drama!"

Faulty Friends

"One of the most beautiful qualities of true friendship is to understand and to be understood."
— Lucius Annaeus Seneca

Faulty friends are the ones who don't have your back. They're the ones who are your friend one minute and not the next. Or maybe they're your friend at certain times and not other times. Maybe they've started rumors about you, talked behind your back, or even flirted with your girlfriend or boyfriend right in front of you. In short, they are untrustworthy and not a real friend.

Let me ask you, are you a good friend? If so, don't you think you deserve others to be a good friend to you? If you're treating others nicely and caring about them, you deserve that in return.

If you've had a bad situation happen with a friend, don't de-friend them for life and cut them off instantly, but instead, give them time and space, be compassionate, and caring. And, at the same time, know your values and have high standards for yourself.

People can change, so allow them to. But if they continue to be a "faulty friend," you have to give yourself permission to let them go. It's easy to get caught up with these kinds of friends because you swear they're a good person, they're your friend, and you don't understand why they are being the way they are, but after a while, you gotta stand up for yourself and know that you deserve better.

Yeah, everyone makes mistakes, I get it, but if it's happening over and over again, you have to get a clue — it's time for you to let them go. Forgiveness is essential and maybe you will be friends again someday, but right now you gotta break the ties.

Once you let them go, wish them the best in your heart. Take time to remember all the fun times you had and enjoy feeling good about the past. This will help to fully let go and move forward, opening up new doors and possibilities for yourself.

Have high standards for yourself. Be patient, be picky, and trust that you will find your tribe.

"Stick with the people who pull the magic out of you,
not the madness."
— Author unknown

The Blame Game

"Happiness depends upon ourselves." — Aristotle

Sammy came running in from the playground. "She doesn't want to play with me. She should! I'm her friend," came screaming out of her mouth. After taking a few deep breaths, getting some water, and calming down, she came back to me to talk.

She calmly restated, "My feelings are hurt because she doesn't want to play with me today."

It was as simple as that. She turned it around, owned her emotions, and used an "I statement" to express herself. I was an elementary-school teacher for a few years and quickly learned the importance of "I statements" from these little kids. If elementary kids can do it, we should all be able to, right?

Pointing the finger at the other person and blaming them for how we feel is an easy way out, but it's not the right way out.

As I learned from these youngsters, it's important to get in touch with what the problem is, not who the problem is. The source of the pain is usually how what happened made us feel.

When you can figure out how the person or situation makes you feel, then use an "I statement," just like Sammy did. It's about owning our feelings rather than blaming others for what they did or didn't do.

A Game Changer

Here is a simple equation to help you change the outcomes of situations:

$$E + R = O \qquad \text{Event} + \text{Response} = \text{Outcome}$$

The event is the event, it doesn't change, but the response to the event is up to you. If you want a different outcome, you have to change your response.

Here are some examples:

Example #1

E = Ethan is angry at his parents because they won't get him a new phone.

R1 = Ethan punches the wall.

O = No new phone and he has to pay to fix the wall.

Different Response, Different Outcome

R2 = Ethan asks what he can do to get a new phone. He's open to conversation and negotiation. He stays calm and is respectful.

O = A better chance of getting a phone sooner than later.

Example #2

E = Emily is frustrated because she can't play in the next basketball game. She missed too many practices. She told the coach it wasn't her fault but he didn't care.

R1 = Emily kicks the water bottles over and walks out of practice.

O = Emily missed playing in two games because of her behavior and had to do extra sprints at the end of practice the next day.

Different Response, Different Outcome

R2 = Emily takes responsibility for her actions. She owns the fact that she was late and recognizes that being on time for practice is a rule of the team. She shows up at the game as a team supporter and gets to practice on time from now on.

O = Emily's teammates appreciate her support during the game and she gets to play in the next one.

Example #3

E = Lilly is upset because Mark broke up with her.

R1 = Lilly cried all day and wouldn't let anyone in her room. She didn't want to talk to anyone about it. She stayed in bed all day.

O = Lilly felt terrible and didn't sleep at all. She missed all her classes the next day, including her math final that she now has to make up.

Different Response, Different Outcome

R2 = Lilly talks to a trusted adult and lets all her emotions out. Then does something fun with a friend to get her mind off things.

O = Lilly feels better, relaxed, but still sad. She knows she has people who care about her and are there to support her.

Example #4

E = Ashton is mad because his parents are getting a divorce.

R1 = Ashton speeds off in his car to go hang with his friends.

O = Ashton ignores his parents' calls and texts. He gets home late and his parents take away his car keys for a week.

<u>Different Response, Different Outcome</u>

R2 = Ashton goes to his uncle's house to talk. Ashton realizes that he doesn't want his life to change. He gets all his emotions out and realizes that he's afraid of how his parent's divorce is going to change his life. His uncle is a good listener and allows Ashton to talk through it all.

O = Ashton feels better because he got all the weight of his emotions off his chest. After he talks with his uncle, he meets up with friends. He lets his parents know where he is and when he'll be home. He gets to keep his car keys.

Every response that we have leads to an outcome, an outcome that we like or don't like. Reckless, abusive, reactionary behavior just makes things worse. If you don't like the outcome you're getting, take a look at your response to the situation and then see if you want to change it. It's all up to you.

Permission to Play

*"Fifteen, there's never a wish better than this when
you only got hundred years to live."*
— Five for Fighting, *100 Years* song lyrics

Red gingham vinyl covered two foldable tables in the
middle of the garage. Deviled eggs with a dusting of
paprika lay in a circular serving dish in the middle, each
one having a home of their own. Bags of potato and corn
chips, a rectangular dish of taco dip, and a platter with lines
of ham, turkey, and swiss cheese lay to the left with a big
bowl of round sandwich buns next to it.

Adults sat and stood, talking endlessly about the
weather, their children, and the news.

Being nineteen, it wasn't the most thrilling place to be.

I looked to my right, out to a field of grass and spied
my younger cousin and four friends playing on the
playground. Watching one run after the other up the slide
then down the slide, their laughter woke the inner dread in
me. Slumped over in my chair, I turned back and looked at
the circle of adults, hearing the same conversations over
and over again.

I stood up, turned around, and ran out to the
playground. A smile soon dawned as I began to chase all
five kids up and down the slide, tagging their arms between
the chains of the swings, and zig-zagging between the
wooden posts. Together, we laughed and screamed our way
through the day.

There is no age limit to being a kid. Being nineteen, I
felt like my only choice was to hang out with the adults but

that wasn't really where I wanted to be. It wasn't fun for me. Playing with the kids was definitely the best option.

It seems like stress and seriousness of school, competitions, jobs, homework, college applications, and various other responsibilities can take over your life. Make sure to always, no matter your responsibilities, laugh, be silly, play, and have fun.

The American Psychological Association did a study in 2014 showing teens' stress level was equivalent to adults' stress level[8]. That's crazy! Play needs to be a part of everyone's life. Life can get busy, but try your best not to forget what brings you joy and happiness.

What fun things do you like to do? Are you making time to do those things?

No matter how hefty your goals, in order to achieve them you have to have balance. Go play on a playground, swing, dance, finger paint, sing your heart out, have fun, laugh. No matter what, remember to always be a kid.

---

[8] http://www.apa.org/news/press/releases/2014/02/teen-stress.aspx

9

Power Sources

Power & True Power - What's the Difference?

Most people think Power is:

- Money
- Having lots of friends
- Wearing cool clothes
- Driving an awesome car
- Having a gazillion likes and followers on Twitter and Instagram
- Living in a big house
- Being invited to the party
- Going to the college of your dreams

But, these things only create temporary happiness — it only lasts for so long before you're wanting something else or something more to make you happy again. It's like getting a new shirt. It's cool at first, you love wearing it, but after a couple weeks, it's in the back of your closet and you forget you even have it. Now you want something else, a new shirt, the new trend, whatever it is that will make you feel good.

Most people live this way. It's their pattern. They buy things, do things, and post things to make themselves happy, to feel good about themselves. It only lasts so long, then they have to buy something else, do something else, post something else to get that feel-good feeling inside, that dopamine chemical going in the brain, once more — a never-ending process, never bringing lasting happiness.

When I was a teenager, friends were my source of happiness. All I wanted to do was hang out with them. When they weren't around, I'd watch TV, which was a good replacement, but a temporary fix, just like my friends were. Nothing seemed to replace that alone feeling I had deep inside.

True Power is:

Self-Love
Happiness
Joy
Peace Inside
Inner Knowing

True Power is inside of you, it's not something you find outside of yourself. It doesn't come from your parents, boyfriends, girlfriends, cats, dogs, or even ferrets. So many people feel they need others, outside of themselves, to survive and to thrive, but you already have all you need inside of you; you are your own source of love. No person or thing can give you the amount of love you already have inside of yourself.

Your purpose in life is to share your love, to serve, and to have fun - not to sulk, suffer, or sit around waiting for life to happen. When you have peace inside, you'll have peace outside. When you share your love and strengths with others, you'll feel it in your heart and love more.

We need you 100%. Living in True Power is the ultimate goal. You'll find your way — not someone else's, but your own. You are the one.

Power Depleters & Power Enhancers

"Hold, hold on, hold onto me 'cause I'm a little unsteady." — X Ambassadors, *Unsteady* song lyrics

Power Depleters

Power Depleters create pain, suffering, and separation. They suck away your energy, making you feel like you're in prison and unable to have any kind of success or happiness in your life. They are the cause of low self-esteem and hopelessness, blocking your creative spirit.

stress	judgement	stuffed emotions	making up stories
gossip	complaining	negative self-talk	limiting thoughts and beliefs
doubt	procrastination	avoidance	believing others before yourself
fear	blaming others	family frustration	not taking responsibility
drama	self-denial	excessive thinking	comparing

Common Power Depleters:

Out of all the Power Depleters listed, what would you say are your top three right now? You could have more than three, but what are the big ones?

_____

_____

_____

Are you willing to let them go? If so, when? If not, why? What are you getting from holding on to them?

Put all of your Power Depleters in a big imaginary balloon in front of you and let go of the string, letting the Universe take them away.

Power Enhancers

Power Enhancers create peace, happiness, and freedom. They give you energy, raise your self-esteem, self-confidence, and allow your creativity to flourish.

forgiveness	kindness	action	being helpful
appreciation	quiet time	service	positive thoughts & beliefs
positivity	discipline	listening	making wise choices
gratitude	movement	faith	sharing feelings and emotions
responsibility	compassion	resiliency	understanding

<u>Common Power Enhancers:</u>

What are three Power Enhancers you are willing to start having, being, and doing right now?

_____

_____

_____

Power Enhancers help you live a life based on your values with peace, happiness, and freedom in your heart. Between now and the end of the book, I share some power enhancers that have worked for me and many others. See if you are willing to use some of them for yourself.

Gratitude

"Expect nothing and appreciate everything."
— Unknown

Gratitude can shift your mood instantaneously and bring you back to what's going on right here, right now. It's easy to get caught up in all that is bad, negative, or what you don't like. I definitely lived in that space a long time. But acknowledging what you're grateful for on a daily basis can help change your focus from bad to good, from negative to positive. Doing this little thing can really change your life.

Every morning and every night, list the things you are thankful for. It could be as simple as, "Thank you for a bed to sleep in," "Thank you for a day off of school," or, "Thank you for the life that I have."

You can even thank yourself. For example, maybe you had a moment of total frustration with someone. You can say, "Thank you for staying calm" to yourself. Remember to keep it positive. You may have wanted to say, "Thank you for staying calm even though I really wanted to lose it on her," but, "Thank you for staying calm," and leaving out the rest, "Even though I really wanted to lose it on her," would work better.

You don't have to say it out loud, you can say it in your head; you can use "thankful," "grateful," you decide. It's whatever you're comfortable with. You can also write it down. Some teens get a notebook or journal and write what they're grateful for every night before they go to bed.

I used to have a small notebook by my bed and before I went to sleep, I took time to write what I was grateful for that day. Now, I just go through it in my head when I lie down at night and when I wake up in the morning before getting up. It's as simple as, "Thank you for warm blankets, a good night's sleep, good friends, a fun day ahead, the ease of writing;" or whatever it is for that day.

What are you grateful for?

Love Who You Are

"I want to be the person who feels great in her body and can say that she loves it and doesn't want to change anything." — Emma Watson

Magazines, TV, the internet, Instagram, and other social-media sites are all right in front of you with someone or something to compare yourself to. That is when the self-abuse and self-sabotage begin to play in your head. You start to compare yourself to others, slowly putting yourself down or building yourself up at the expense of others.

"I wish I were tall like her," "I'm fat," "I want shoes like theirs." Some take it to the opposite extreme by putting others down to make them feel good, but deep down inside they are just as insecure as everyone else.

Your body is your home. It's where you live. Do you take care of it? Do you nurture it and show it love? Or, do you abuse it and put it down?

You and each person in this world is unique — on purpose. That's the gift of all of us — that we have characteristics and qualities we get to call our own. You are you. I am me. You were born perfect just like me.

I'll admit, this area is not my strength. I can be pretty good at verbal self-abuse and put-downs. It's something I've worked on my entire life. However, I've come to realize the importance of embracing the imperfections and the perfections within myself and believe we all need to start doing that. On the next page, you're going to start naming all of the amazing qualities and characteristics of yourself.

If you have a hard time with these exercises, think about what other people like and say about you. What do your friends, family, or even strangers compliment you on?

It may or may not be hard to talk about yourself and see the awesomeness in you, but it's there and give yourself permission to love it a little, even a lot!

114

"My definition of stupid is wasting your opportunity to be yourself, because I think everybody has a uniqueness and everybody's good at something." — Pink

Let's begin by naming all the qualities and characteristics you like about your body. Is it your lanky legs or stubby toes? What about your hair? Your face? Your nails? Your elbows? Go through every part of your body and recognize what's awesome about you physically.

_____

_____

_____

_____

_____

_____

Now, think about the qualities and characteristics of your personality. Who are you? What do you like about yourself? Is it your silliness? Your loud laugh? Your shyness?

_____

_____

_____

_____

_____

_____

_____

What are your strengths and hobbies? What are you good at and proud of?

_____

_____

_____

_____

_____

_____

Now it's time to own it. Take all of what you wrote above and put it below. Write it, draw it, doodle it, scribble it, whatever you gotta do — get it all out — right here, right now!

Once you have your list or collage of self loves, go to a mirror, look yourself in the eye and read them to yourself. This is no time to be shy. Own it.

I LOVE MY _____.
I AM _____.
YES, I AM.

OWN YOUR AWESOMENESS!

If you can, do this exercise every day and notice the love within yourself wake up. You'll soon begin to believe those words — if you don't already!

Now, protect it, honor it, and care for it. Take pride in your body and yourself. It's yours and nobody else's. Don't let others hurt you in any way, physically, mentally, or emotionally. You and your body are yours and you are the permission-giver for it.

Love you.

Love being you.

Collecting Compliments

"When I see your face, there's not a thing I would change 'cause girl you're amazing, just the way you are." — Bruno Mars

Compliments are a good thing, right?

So if they are, why are so many of us terrible at receiving and loving them up?! We either nudge them off, responding with a nod or possibly a "Yeah," or maybe act like we didn't even hear them.

Maybe some of you have nagging parents that constantly make you say "Thank you" when anyone says anything good about you so you were raised to say thank you, but you may not believe it.

Half of accepting a compliment is receiving it. The other half is believing it. Believing you're awesome and full of love is numero uno to high self-worth and True Power.

Below you'll see four responses to a compliment. The first is full of resistance and denial. The last one is complete acceptance. Where are you within the stages of receiving a compliment?

Four Stages of Receiving a Compliment:

1. **Complete resistance:**
   Blow it off, don't even hear it.
2. **Partial resistance:**
   Say, "Yeah," then walk away, knowing something was said but you have no idea what it was.
3. **Partial acceptance:**
   Say, "Thanks," then walk away, not thinking much of it.
4. **Complete acceptance:**
   Say, "Thanks" or "Thank you," really take it in and believe, feeling the goodness in you.

What about you? Do you resist compliments or totally accept them, loving the goodness of being you?

"When I say to you, there is nobody like me, and there never was, that is a statement I want every woman to feel and make about themselves." — Lady Gaga

Direct and Honest Communication

"The single biggest problem in communication is the illusion that it has taken place."
— George Bernard Shaw

Communication is an exchange of information, in hopes to connect, be heard, and to be understood. Being direct and honest, saying exactly what you want to say, using facts, opinions, and "I statements," and not skirting around the issue usually works best.

A lot of communication is done through text, tweets, posts, and hashtags these days; however, I want to teach you how having clear thoughts and messages can benefit you.

ASH
I listened patiently as Ash downloaded. I could tell that Ash was frustrated by the tone in her voice, the heavy sigh before she spoke, and the hunched-over body she had. She rattled off everything that bothered her about her BFF, the one that she had only good things to say about two weeks ago.

Ash wanted to break up with her best friend. She didn't want only one friend anymore; she felt like Viv, her BFF, was holding her back. They were going to be seniors and Ash wanted to make sure she enjoyed her senior year.

When I showed up for our meeting, Ash had been texting back and forth with Viv all day long. She talked to her several times on the phone and in person during the week, but Viv just didn't get it. She could not understand why Ash, all of a sudden, didn't want to be friends with her any longer.

She had been feeling smothered and wanted a break from hanging out with Viv, but I also felt such heartache for Viv.

Ash showed me the string of texts that had gone back and forth with Viv that day. Now I understood why Viv was so confused. There was never a clear message from Ash stating exactly how she felt, what she wanted, or needed out of the friendship.

I gave Ash time to think of what she wanted from Viv and for their friendship. I also asked her what it would be like if Viv did this to her. How would she feel?

With compassion and a lot of questioning, Ash finally figured it out. Together, we composed a text that clearly stated how she felt, what she could and could not give to the friendship, and what she wanted for the future of their friendship.

It was hard for Ash to be honest and direct, but she did it. She texted complete sentences and told Viv exactly how she felt, realizing how heartbreaking it would be for Viv to receive.

How would you want to be communicated with if you were on the other end of the situation?

When it comes to matters of the heart, clear communication is always the best way to go. It's the only way to be respectful of the other person and the situation at hand. Always take time to think about the other person and how it is for them.

> *"If you want others to be happy, practice compassion.*
> *If you want to be happy, practice compassion."*
> — the Dalai Lama

Winning with Parents

> *"I can do things you cannot, you can do things I cannot; Together, we can do great things."*
> — Mother Teresa

Your mother and father are your first teachers. You learn everything from them, from how to hold a fork to the words you speak. When they aren't doing your laundry, cooking you a meal, or giving you money, they're irritating you because of what they said or didn't say, did or didn't do, or what they will or will not let you do.

Parents can definitely be a problem. They say, "No" when you want them to say, "Yes." They have rules you don't agree with, and sometimes, they like to embarrass you in front of your friends.

As much as you want to, you can't change them. You may complain about them, yell about them, walk away, slam doors, and blame them for your terrible life, but that's not going to help. You have to let them be them and you be you.

Some parents feel they always have to have the last word. Some always feel they are right. Do you ever fight for the last word or feel that you're always right and they're always wrong?

It would be nice if parents would get it, accept that you do know a lot, listen instead of interrupting all the time, and realize you can be right and not always wrong, but that's not always the case.

To be the bigger person means giving up the fight and letting the other person be right. It's about letting them have the last word and just letting it go. It's not always easy to do, but if you decide to, you'll have more peace and less frustration in your life.

> *"It's not always rainbows and butterflies,*
> *it's compromise that moves us along."*
> — Maroon 5

Parents can be hard to talk to, but you have to remember that parents are people, too. I'm sure you didn't want to hear that, but it's true. They can be frustrating and annoying at times, but believe it or not, they are trying their best. A win-win situation can happen between you and your parents if and only if you start by doing the following:

5 Steps to Succeeding with Parents:

1 Pick a Good Time to Talk
- Don't attempt to speak with them when you or they are running out the door or when they just get home from work.

2 Remain Calm
- Remaining calm could be the hardest thing to do but it's the most important.
- Breathe through any anger, disapproval, or annoyance you may have.
- Leave the area if you must, but don't say or do anything unless you're in a calm state.
- You have to be in a calm state in order to move forward with the next steps.

3 Be the Bigger Person
- Listen to what they are saying.
- If you tend to interrupt with, "Yeah, but" all the time, don't.
- You may want to roll your eyes, but don't.
- You may want to clench your teeth, but don't.
- Have an open mind, listen to what they have to say, and try your best to understand their point of view.
  - Don't sit and pretend to listen, blocking them out with your thoughts of how they are wrong and you disagree 110% with everything they are saying. That will get you nowhere.

- Nod a few times, say a few "Okays," not to agree per se, but to show them you are listening.
- Imagine you are them in this situation. I know, it's not something you really want to do, but it's the only way to have an adult conversation and to negotiate any type of agreement that you will be happy with.
- If they knew how to do this, they would, but you are going to be their teacher right now.
- If your parents don't give you any information nor have a reason for their decision, then ask them, "Can you please tell me what's so bad about _____?" or "Can you give me a reason why so I can understand where you're coming from?"

- Watch your tone of voice. If you have a whiny tone or a hint of complaint in your voice, they won't like it and you'll be starting a war, which is the last thing you want. You want to speak with respect.

I'm not guaranteeing they'll believe that you want to have a respectful conversation, but you can try. Often times, you may be met with the answer, "It's not good for you," or worse, "Because I said so." That gets you nowhere and leaves you totally powerless.

The goal is to have an adult-like conversation in hopes of feeling good about it and to have a win-win situation for both you and your parents.

4 Take Your Turn

- Hopefully you got an explanation or reason of some sort.
- Now say, "Can I share my side of the story?" or "Can I talk now?" — something like that, but in your own words. (Remember, watch your tone of voice!)
- Tell them how you feel.
- Never, never point the finger at them or act disrespectfully.
- Only use "I statements." For example, "I think it's fair for me because _____."

This is your time to negotiate. Whatever it is you want, try to be reasonable. You know your parents better than I do. Start small then go big. If you start big, they may not go for it right away. But, then again, you know your parents, you decide what's best.

It's up to you to respect them so they will respect you.

5 Propose a Solution

- "I'd like to _____. What do you think?" or "I'd like to propose a solution, _____."
- Be specific. Most parents like specificity. The more details, the better. You know they're going to ask a ton of questions, so be clear the first time.

By practicing this way of communicating, you not only exercise your young-adult rights, you're preparing yourself for future relationships and parent negotiations.

Focus on the Good

"Most folks are as happy as they make up their minds to be." — Abraham Lincoln

English was always my worst subject. My teacher's favorite saying was, "You're rude, crude, and socially unacceptable," which, being seniors, we probably were! I, like a lot of my classmates, focused on everything we hated about that class: all the homework, the end-of-the-year term paper we had to do, and the fact that it was the last class of the day. Although I frequently complained about that class, by the end of the year, I actually learned a lot.

There are always things we don't want to do in life, like homework, studying, taking a certain class, maybe school in general, but it's a reality that we have to do certain things to get to where we want to go, and school is one of them.

In life, you can either focus on what you like or don't like, what's going well or not well, what you want or don't want. It's all a game and you are the only player in your life who can make a difference by what you put your focus on.

Your mind can easily fixate on all the things you hate in your life, causing you to go into a downward spiral of depression. Or, you can start seeing and feeling the good in your life.

Norman Vincent Peale says, "Change your thoughts and you change your world." What are your thoughts? Do they focus on the bad or the good? How do you want to experience life?

How could you use your time to better yourself in some way? You can sit, bored out of your mind, and complain, or choose to do something about it. You can decide to learn something new every day or not. Whether it's a new fact about the world, a new word, or how to stay awake when you keep nodding off during class — whatever it is, the choice is yours.

Relationships, communication skills, social skills, emotions, feelings, money, health – it's all part of your life education. The world is your classroom. Decide on what you want to learn and find the people or resources to learn from. It's all out there, all you have to do is ask.

10
Real Life Stuff

Family Realities

"I guess we are who we are for a lot of reasons. And maybe we'll never know most of them. But even if we don't have the power to choose where we come from, we can still choose where we go from there." — movie quote, *The Perks of Being a Wallflower*

I sat cross-legged on the soft brown textured carpet, three feet in front of the television screen. The aroma of meatloaf drifted from the kitchen fifteen feet away. The plates and silverware rang as my mom set the table.

Just as I laughed at Arnold, a black boy on one of my favorite TV shows, the solid wood front door opened. Sitting up straight, I quickly hid my smile. My dad walked between me and the T.V., breaking my gaze. His heavy, manure-laden leather boots stepped inches from me, while his right hand swooped down and grasped the plastic black knob with his thumb and index finger, like he was turning the key to the front door. Off went Different Strokes and on went some other show with white people on it.

I pushed the small black button in, turning off the T.V., and walked to my room, defeated and angry that I couldn't watch what I wanted to and because of the unfairness in my life, not understanding why.

I never agreed with the limitations and rules I was raised with regarding situations like this, but now understand why I am the way I am.

Growing up in a rural area, I craved the diversity it was lacking. I dreamed of another life, a life with all kinds of people, different cultures and languages. Whenever we had an exchange student in our school, I clung to them for any outside exposure I could get.

My life path has included traveling and living in other countries, living in various cities in the U.S., having friends of different nationalities and cultures, speaking another language, and volunteering for organizations with diverse populations. With all of this, I've come to realize the benefit of my childhood experiences and my own values for life.

I am who I am because of everything in my past. It hasn't been easy. It's taken a lot of self-work and time to let go of anger, resentment, and bitterness, but I've come to learn that those three forms of hate are just big orange and black roadblocks that got in the way of me doing any good in this world.

Now I'm able to celebrate what was, what is, and what will be, and taking time to be thankful for everything that has ever been given to me — the love, the money, and the support from various people in various ways. It may not have come in the package I wanted it to, but none the less, it has helped form who I am today.

What about you?

Can you see how your experiences have benefited you? Can you see that you are loved even though it may not look or feel the way you would like it to? Do you have any anger, resentment, and hurt going on in your life? Are you willing to let it go in order for you to be happier in life?

Stupid Kids

"The only true currency in this bankrupt world is the truth that we share with one another when we are being uncool." — movie quote, *Almost Famous*

The fans above dispersed the smell of fresh ground coffee beans in the air. Like incense, it lingered in the space above people's heads as they sat and chatted over coffee, tea, and freshly baked scones. Two gentlemen sat to my right, one dressed in cycling shorts and shirt, his feet clicked as he walked by in his silver and white road-bike shoes. The other was dressed in faded blue jeans, white sneakers, and a beige Polo sweater with a blue and red plaid cotton shirt underneath.

It was like they were meeting in their kitchen or something; the local newspaper sat on the round table in front of them, along with two coffee mugs full of dark roast. Sitting back in their plastic, yellow chairs, they filled each other in on family, life, and world happenings.

Sitting three feet to my right, I couldn't help but listen to bits and pieces of their not-so-quiet conversation. Between them, the clanking of the espresso machine, and the roaring jazz music, it made for a very noisy and distracting work environment — not a good day to forget my headphones!

Tuning in and out of my work, "teenage drinking" caught my attention. I soon got from the two men's discussion that a kid got caught drinking and smoking before school.

"That's just plain stupid, if you ask me," the biker guy stated.

The other guy responded, "Oh, that was always happening at Bennington High. Don't you remember?"

I wish I could say that I was smarter than the kid they were talking about, but I was stupid, too.

Kids like that get labeled "troubled." According to www.merriam-webster.com, troubled is defined as: "exhibiting emotional or behavioral problems." Matrona on UrbanDictionary.com says that troubled is: "Mentally disturbed as a result of reckless behavior (Drug use, Alcohol, Excessive Partying), or by Depression, Anxiety/Break from reality due to traumatic experiences. Or, one of the aforementioned causing the other."

So, if that's the case, why wasn't I labeled a "troubled kid?"

The only reason why is because I didn't get caught. Like many teenagers out there, I hid it well. I played the part. I looked like every other kid who wouldn't be doing that kind of stuff, but did.

So, how many more "troubled kids" are out there who keep it hidden just like I did? Doing drugs, cutting, drinking, lying, or whatever else?

Everyone who does all of those things wants love and acceptance just like everyone else. They may feel depressed, confused, and lost, but that doesn't mean they don't care about life. They want to live; they just may not know how.

Is this you? Or, do you know someone like this?

We all hurt in some way but we deal with it in different ways. Some cover it up. Some wear it on their sleeve. Some let everyone know about it through social media.

Can you help someone find the good within themselves? Seeing beyond outer appearances, stopping the gossip, and asking how you can help is the answer. Compassion is key.

How can you step into life and make good things happen?

Hurtful Humans

"Darkness cannot drive out darkness; only light can do that. Hate cannot drive out hate; only love can do that." — Martin Luther King, Jr.

Mia Madison was her name. She plowed through the hallways, not caring if you were a boy or a girl, older or younger. She got through and took everyone down with her. Boys screeched, "Ouch!" as their shoulder slammed against the apricot-colored wall.

Humans can be pretty hurtful toward others. Known as bullies; hurtful humans can cause harm physically, emotionally, and mentally. They can be a boy, a girl, a man, a woman, a parent, friend, teacher, or sibling. Age, class, and physical appearance doesn't matter.

People are not born to be hurtful toward others: they learn it. Most likely, these hurtful humans have been hurt or bullied by someone else at some point in their lives and, as a result, develop hate and resentment within themselves and then repeat the hurtful behavior toward others.

Words can hurt as much as a punch or slap. The only way to create change is to dissolve the hate — and it all starts with you.

How do you treat others?

I know that I distanced myself from Mia in school. I wanted nothing to do with her. I may even have put out negative vibes toward her. Instead of being nice, I was cold and distant.

Some other kids got to know her. They broke the barrier of harshness and after a few months, we began to see a smile on her face and a laugh as she walked down the halls. She wasn't as mean as she used to be.

I watched as others got to know her and let her into their circle of friends. I started to put down my wall of self-protection as well and began to smile when I saw her instead of shunning her, scrunching up my nose.

I was not the first one to change the dynamics of this hurtful human, but I observed and learned from others. I started to treat her like I would have wanted to be treated and little by little, the fear disappeared. How are you treating others?

We're born to love, not hate.

Stage Fright and Fear

"Excellence is never an accident. It is always the result of high intention, sincere effort, and intelligent execution; it represents the wise choice of many alternatives – choice, not chance, determines your destiny." — Aristotle

I sat in the back, with two rows of students behind me. The auditorium was a little over half-full. Seniors sat in the front rows in the left, center, and right sections. Juniors, sophomores, and freshman followed. The stage in front housed six speech contestants sitting in tan, metal folding chairs, with space surrounding them and garnet velvet curtains hanging on the far right and left sides. The musty odor consumed the oversized space.

One by one, the speech contestants walked to the left side of the stage. Stepping up on the podium, they were six inches higher in order to see their young faces. They placed their notecards on the wooden lectern, took a deep breath, and began.

The rows of high school students surrounding me responded in various ways to each speech. Some remained slouched in the red cushioned seats with their chins resting on their chests the entire time; some fell asleep, while others sat up straight listening to every word.

Thunderous clapping stirred the room as each person finished.

Ten-seconds in, the sixth speaker began to wake the crowd. The sleepers and slouchers giggled and opened their eyes to see who was so funny. We all oohed and awed our way through the presentation. I watched in admiration of her confidence and poised nature.

Clearly winning the contest that day, she commanded and captivated the 364 students in the audience.

Confidence is the belief in your own internal powers, that True Power inside of you. It's when you access your True Power and allow it to lead the way. She definitely had it.

Fear is the opposite. It's when you're full of worry, doubt, and anxiety. It's the disbelief of your internal powers. Fear is the result of you not accessing your True Power and, instead, trying to control the outcome.

> *"Whatever fear I have inside me,*
> *my desire to win is always stronger."*
> — Serena Williams

Speaking in front of others was always difficult for me. As much as I dreamed to be on stage, singing and acting, I could never get over my fear of doing it. Even in a class of just twenty students, a heavy palpitation consumed my chest and blocked my voice from coming through.

If we were going around the room answering questions during class, all I could do was rehearse my answer over and over again in my head until it was finally my turn to get it out. When it was my turn to present in front of the class, my hands and voice would quiver like strummed guitar strings. It was a truly horrific experience for me.

Believe it or not, improv classes were the best way for me to overcome my fear of speaking in front of others.

How is fear holding you back? What can you do to overcome your fear?

Fear shows up in many ways, from speaking in front of others to asking someone to the prom. It's all the same. With practice, trust, and a deep desire to try, you will be able to conquer your fear just like I did.

11
Let It Go

Patience, Understanding, & Appreciation

"Do, or do not. There is no try."
— Yoda, *Star Wars: Episode V - The Empire Strikes Back*

<u>Patience</u>

"Just give it to me!" my nephew exclaimed. His thin pale body squirmed in the seat ahead of me like a baby bird trying to break free from the hard shell he had called home for the last twelve days. His hand reached toward his dad time and time again, retracting once more with unfed hunger inside.

"Just a second!" his dad replied repeatedly, "I have to send this text. Be patient!"

I sat in the backseat watching all this go down.

Although it seemed like eternity for my nephew, it was probably a whole two minutes of waiting. However long it was, it wasn't easy for anyone in that moment.

Patience is all about being calm in the moment. There are some people who are so mellow about everything — they pretty much define patience for everyone. Then, there are others that spaz out and can't wait a second for anything. I definitely think this whole ADHD thing is part of this, which I have a little inside of me, too.

Usually, if I'm being impatient, my heart starts to race and I can feel it pounding in my chest. What's worked is to slow down, pause in the moment, and feel the beating of my heart. It brings me back to what's going on inside of me and around me.

What about you? How patient are you? It could be waiting for the light to turn green, the barista at Starbucks to give you your latte, or your mom or dad to reply to your text. Do you get antsy and impatient with yourself and others or are you pretty mellow and generally patient with people and situations around you?

<u>Understanding</u>

We all stood encircling our friend, Ally. Tears dripped from behind her hands as they covered her small face. Thomas had just broken up with her. We hugged and listened to her as she wept in sadness. After maybe five minutes, Tori yelled out, "Hey, let's all go to my house!" and we all turned, picked up our backpacks, and walked in a line taking up the whole sidewalk. Samantha began to rap and one by one, our bodies started to groove. Smiles and laughter followed.

It's easy to get caught up in our own stuff and not even think of others or their point of view, but taking a moment to feel what the other person is feeling is true human connection. Understanding is seeing and feeling things from the other person's point of view. It's a huge part of communication and relationships, yet we can easily get caught up in our own stuff and not even think of others.

How understanding are you of others? Do you take time to think of others and how it is for them?

<u>Appreciation</u>

Appreciation is honoring a characteristic or quality in another person. It's telling them what you appreciate about them, such as, "I appreciate your kindness," "I appreciate your help," or "I appreciate your honesty." We don't use appreciation that often but, like understanding, it's a huge part of communication and relationships. Saying these simple phrases to others and to yourself is such a nice thing to do. It's an easy way to lift someone up and make them, and you, feel good about themselves and life. It's a simple gift, just like listening, to give to another person.

What do you appreciate in life? What do you appreciate about your family? Your friends? Do you ever tell them?

Patience, understanding and appreciation are three elements that can bring more peace and happiness into your life.

"Kind words can be short and easy to speak, but their echoes are truly endless."
— Mother Teresa

Everyone Makes Mistakes

"Out beyond ideas of wrongdoing and right doing, there is a field. Meet me there." — Rumi

Here's an equation that you may like, math not required: Mis + Take = Mistake

Mistakes are mis-takes, like when they make a movie. The producer shouts, "Take One," until there is a mistake, then they holler, "Cut." Minutes later, they try again, "Take Two." This goes on and on until the actors get it right.

Life is like a movie. You get as many "Takes" as you need until you get it right. Some things will take minutes to get, while others could take months or years. But, what counts is that you keep trying, keep going, and keep learning.

The key to moving forward in life is to learn lessons along the way. For every mistake, there is a lesson to be learned.

For example, do you ever say something then walk away and knock yourself in the head, asking yourself, "Why did I say that?! That's so not what I wanted to say." Then the forever beating yourself up goes on and on, obsessing about what you should have said instead.

We mess up all the time in so many different ways. Obsessing about it doesn't make it go away, but realizing it was a mis-take and knowing that you get another "Take" next time certainly helps.

What about you? Have you made any mistakes that you just hang onto and obsess over, wanting things to be different?

Can you see that you made a mis-take and you get another "Take?"

"To help yourself, you must be yourself.
Be the best that you can be.
When you make a mistake, learn from it,
pick yourself up and move on."
— author Dave Pelzer

Forgiveness

"The weak can never forgive. Forgiveness is the attribute of the strong" — Mahatma Gandhi

What I've learned about forgiveness is that it's more about giving yourself freedom than letting the other person off the hook. I thought forgiveness was about giving into the other person and letting them be right and me be wrong, where I'd rather put two fists up high, ready to fight rather than surrender to them being right.

Now I see it differently. I see forgiveness as a tool to use to free myself from any anger, resentment, or disagreement I may have toward another person (or myself). Letting whatever it is go and letting them be them while I be me leaves me with more peace than hate in my life.

Forgiveness allows you to just be, which is what we want but never what we feel. Everyone, including you, is doing their best. Forgiving others for mistakes they have made is so important for living a life of True Power and happiness. Forgiving yourself is even more important for creating the life you want.

Some ways to forgive are: write a letter, have a heart-to-heart conversation, or simply forgive in your mind and move on.

The Ho'oponopono is a simple, yet powerful way to practice forgiveness. It is a Hawaiian forgiveness prayer that has brought many miracles to people's lives. Ho'opono means "to make things right." All you have to do is think of the person or situation that needs to be forgiven and say four short sentences.

The Ho'oponopono, Hawaiian Forgiveness Prayer:
"I'm sorry. Please forgive me. Thank you. I love you."

Keep Going

"Your focus determines your reality." — Qui-Gon Jinn, *Star Wars: Episode I - The Phantom Menace*

Wearing my pastel yellow cotton kurti and white leggings, I walked down the concrete path, lined with square kale-color bushes. The lush green forest of the Himalayas filled the hillside in front of me. Ahead on my left, I saw the three-story apricot and ginger-colored building.

Gazing to my left, I watched a cow standing and gnawing on something in a small fenced-in pasture. With the chaos of the crowded markets in the distance, I lingered down the pathway, no longer able to hear the blaring music bellowing from boom boxes or smell the bouquet of garbage, incense, and sewage.

Returning my gaze forward, my feet slowed their step as my heart stopped and my body stiffened. A chestnut-colored monkey sat solo in the middle of the path in front of me, licking its hand.

Knowing I shouldn't stop, I took a deep breath, exhaled it out slowly, and kept my eyes looking forward. I calmly walked by, imagining in my mind that the monkey would stay in place, undisturbed. I continued on for about eight feet, then leisurely turned my head over my right shoulder, peeking back to check on the whereabouts of the monkey.

Not seeing anything, my whole body turned 180 degrees. Still nothing in sight, I inhaled, turning another 180 degrees. Air seeped out from my tightly wound lips. I shook my head frantically both ways, searching for the monkey.

Then, out of the corner of my left eye, there was movement. I spotted his backside strolling in the open field next door. My chest filled with the biggest inhale I'd ever taken, and exhaled it all out in a big sigh.

Relaxed, I continued on.

> *"He who is not courageous enough to take risks will accomplish nothing in life."*
> — Muhammad Ali

Fear can get the best of us, distracting us from our purpose and path. It's up to you to notice it and have the courage to walk by and keep going in spite of it.

There have been many times I've wanted to quit and did, only to regret it later. I even wanted to quit at times during the writing of this book, but I kept going.

Having the courage to move forward on your path, no matter the distractions or self-sabotage, is the answer.

What do you want?

What are you being guided to do?

Do you have the courage to stay on your path no matter what distractions may be in your way?

"You are braver than you believe, stronger than you seem, and smarter than you think."
— Winnie the Pooh

Let It Go

"Some of us think holding on makes us strong; but sometimes it is letting go." — Hermann Hesse

We've talked a lot already about the weight of problems, drama, and worry that keeps us up at night, distracts us in class, and depletes our energy and True Power. Your mind can make you crazy making up stories, reliving a moment over and over again, and constantly thinking about what you should or shouldn't have done.

I'll share three wise words with you that my gram shared with me: LET IT GO.

What craziness goes on inside your head?

Is there something that you're holding onto that's holding you back and bringing you down?

Are you willing to let go of it?

Release all the craziness from your mind and make room for more important things. The world needs you present and ready to take life on now. The sooner you can let go of the past, the hurts, and the craziness in your mind, the happier you will be to begin again.

Chill Out

"It is not because things are difficult that we do not dare; it is because we do not dare that they are difficult." — Seneca

Nina and Coco are my writing partners, my snugglers, and my all-time faves. Both are Australian Shepherds. Nina is a Black-Tri; Coco is a Blue Merle. Nina loves to hang with dogs; Coco prefers people. Some call them littermates, I call them my kids.

Nina has long black hair with some tan on her back legs, eyebrows, and nose. She has a white stripe up the middle of her forehead, white paws with faint black spots in front, amber eyes, and a white ring around her neck. She sits when you tell her to sit and she comes when you call her.

Coco, on the other hand, doesn't. He has a black and gray splashed coat with white around his neck, legs, paws, and face, and a black patch covering his right eye, accentuating his blue eye on the left and brown eye on the right. He's the dog everyone gravitates to, admiring his beauty.

Coco has a mind of his own. He'll come when he wants to, lie down when he's ready, and go to bed when he's tired. He'll sit, stare, and whine at you until you give him what he wants.

On a walk one day close to our house, we diverted from the main path to a foot-wide dirt trail that leads around to a creek. With two-foot-high golden grass on either side, the three of us walked in single file, Nina in front, Coco in back, and me in the middle. Rounding the corner, I decided it was time to go. Already giving them plenty of times to sniff the grass, I pulled on their leashes as I led them down the trail.

Coco, being Coco, stopped abruptly. All four paws planted into the ground, he leaned his whole body in the opposite direction of me, yanking my left arm back. Whipping my legs around to catch myself, I sighed briefly, rolling my eyes. I looked at Coco standing there determined to make me stop for a moment.

Usually I pull him forward or leave and let him catch up, but today I stopped. I looked at Coco as he slowly turned his head toward the high bare trees and spatter of white across the lapis blue sky, an invitation to follow his gaze. My eyes followed.

Hearing nothing but the soft breeze on the surrounding grass, I took a deep breath in and let it out long and slow, my heart slowing as my eyes and body relaxed. It was like Coco was telling me to chill out or something. I felt peace in the air, in my body, and in the moment.

Teachers come in all shapes and sizes and, on that day, Coco was my teacher. I clearly needed to slow down and chill out. Life can be crazy busy sometimes. Slowing down is the best medicine.

Consider chilling out, Coco style. Slow your body, slow your mind, and take in all the beauty that surrounds you.

Chill Out Coco Style

Slow down
Be still
Breathe it in
Let it out
Enjoy the moment

12

You Are The Answer

True Power

— An intense feeling, underneath the surface, deep within your heart; your inner strength and guidance system.

Access Your True Power

"Silence is a source of great strength." — Lao Tzu

One of my favorite things to do is sit outside at night and look at the stars. I revel in the vast universe in which we live. While everyone else is asleep, the night is quiet. Stillness, even for a moment, fills my heart and soul.

Stillness and quiet are the source of True Power. You want to build and grow quietness inside so you're more able to access your True Power on a regular basis. Sometimes we don't even feel it or hear our True Power, thinking it's not there, but it is. It's usually covered up with busyness and background noise.

It's like strengthening your muscles, like Gram. That first set of arm curls might have been hard on the first day, but when she practiced on a consistent basis, her muscles grew and the arm curls got easier.

When you're in need of help or guidance, all you have to do is tap into your True Power. Get quiet, take a couple breaths, relax, ask your question, wait, allow the answer to come, and trust it's the one for you.

You'll get a feeling, an inner knowing, a hunch from within - that's it! That's your True Power giving you guidance. Trust it. You're the one with your own answers, not someone else.

Accessing Your True Power is just like everything else in life; you've got to practice to get good at it. Practice, cultivate, and embrace it.

3 Must-Haves for True Power:

1 You-Time

- Turn off technology
- Sit, breathe, calm the mind, and relax the body
- Practice the Soup-Can Strength mantra
  - (I matter, my choices matter, no matter what, the world needs me)
- Release control, problems, and struggle
- Let go of busyness, distractions, and drama
- Trust that things will work out

2 You-Love

- Focus on the good
- Forgive yourself
  - Say the Ho'oponopono (I'm sorry. Please forgive me. Thank you. I love you.)
- Have Good Health: Eat healthy food, drink lots of water, get fresh air & exercise
- Sleep at least 7-9 hours every night without any technology nearby
- Live by your Warrior Statement and make choices and decisions that match it
- Play Your True Power Playlist (replace self-sabotage talk with positive talk)
- Own and share your strengths and gifts
- Take responsibility for your life, successes, and happiness

- Be thankful for what you have and who you are
- Allow others to help you
- Celebrate

3 You-Service

- Use kind words
- Act from the heart
- Forgive others: Let Them be Them & You be You
- Realize mistakes are actually Mis-Takes
- Practice patience
- Give the gift of listening
- Understand other people's point of view
- Be polite and helpful

You have all you need deep within your heart.

How will you cultivate, practice, and embrace your True Power?

Service

"The best way to find yourself is to lose yourself in the service of others." — Mahatma Gandhi

It was my job to help pick out clothes, shoes, jewelry, handbags, whatever they needed. I had only known this woman for twenty-five minutes and we sat in the fitting room laughing hysterically with each other. The woman had been homeless in the past and now was ready for a job interview in hopes of changing her life.

Helping others is a great way to keep your mind off your problems. It's the best medicine and it's free! It truly opens your heart and frees your mind, filling you up with love and joy. The feeling of service, no matter what it is, is True Power at its best.

Some ways I've volunteered are:

- Being a youth soccer coach
- Delivering Thanksgiving meals to families in need
- Teaching English to non-English speaking adults
- Helping to build a school playground
- Handing out snacks at a marathon
- Visiting the elderly
- Being a swim angel during a triathlon

Being of service is not only about volunteering your time, but sharing who you are and the gifts you were born with.

How can you be of service to others?

"No act of kindness, no matter how small, is ever wasted."
— Aesop

Everyday Gifts of Service:

- A smile
- Holding the door for someone
- Using kind words
- Shoveling a neighbor's walk
- Having patience and understanding
- Doing the right thing because it's the human thing to do

"Too often we underestimate the power of a touch, a smile, a kind word, a listening ear, an honest compliment, or the smallest act of caring, all of which have the potential to turn a life around." – author Leo Buscaglia

Another way to serve the world is to be of service to yourself. If you're not helping yourself, then you'll eventually feel empty and depleted. Go back to your Life Values and Life Dreams. Which ones excite you? Which ones makes your heart sing?

Sometimes people feel they need permission or approval to be, do, and have grandiosity in life. If that's you, I now give you permission and approval to be, do, and have what you desire and deserve.

Align with your heart and be happy. Serve the world with your greatness. Don't let anyone stand in your way, not even yourself. And, bring peace and love to the world. You matter, your life matters, and we need you.

"Just don't give up trying to do what you really want to do. Where there is love in inspiration, I don't think you can go wrong." — Ella Fitzgerald

Now What?

Many years after my friend died by suicide, there was another suicide in my small town. Now living in a place where education about suicide prevention and depression awareness is taught to middle and high-school students, parents, and people of the community, I was desperate to know if anything had changed since my high-school years. I asked questions but there weren't many answers.

Not many people wanted to talk about it. I finally realized that I needed to be patient and understand that everyone deals with things differently. I believe that we need to educate ourselves on the topic of stress, suicide, and depression, accepting that it's real and we do need to talk about it. We need to talk about and practice new ways of being so we can have freedom and happiness in our lives.

I wrote this book in hopes that it will be a source of help for you. Start the conversation with your friends, and use this book as a guide.

You Are The Answer

"So let the light guide your way, yeah. Hold every memory as you go. And every road you take, will always lead you home, home." — Wiz Khalifa and Charlie Puth, *See You Again* song lyrics

You matter. Your choices matter. No matter what, we need you. When you can start thinking in the positive, you'll start living in the positive.

Most people turn to prescription drugs to cure them of feeling down, stressed out, not happy, and feeling lost in the busy world we live in, but I invite you to try other ways first.

Practice:

- The 3 Must-Haves for True Power
- Play your True Power Playlist in your mind over and over
- Chill Out Coco Style
- Learn to let things go, de-stress, and receive compliments
- Change the outcome by changing your response
- Use the 7 Steps to Ease the Pain
  and most importantly, **LOVE YOURSELF**.

I know you can do this. I believe in you. You were born with a sparkle in your eye and laughter that fills the room.

Being you 100% is all you have to be. Use this book to strengthen your True Power, live powerfully, love, and be of service to the world.

You got this!

With love and light in my heart,
thank you for allowing me to be your guide.
~ Mary Lynne

Stay Connected!

Instagram: @MaryLynneFernandez
Twitter: @Mary_Lynne
Facebook: @MaryLynneSpeaks

My Life Values & Life Dreams
Today's date: _____

My Life Values:

_____

_____

_____

_____

_____

My Life Dreams:

_____

_____

_____

_____

_____

My Warrior Statement:

_____

_____

_____

_____

In addition to the warning signs for depression, I also want to include the warning signs for suicide. Below are the warning signs for suicide, if you see these signs in yourself or someone you know, please call the National Suicide Prevention Lifeline at 1-800-273-TALK (8255) or find a trusted adult who can get you the help you need.

Remember, you matter, your life matters, and we need you!

<u>American Foundation for Suicide Prevention
Suicide Warning Signs[9]</u>

People who are considering suicide often display one or more of the following moods:
- Depression
- Anxiety
- Loss of interest
- Irritability
- Humiliation
- Agitation
- Rage

If a person talks about:
- Killing themselves
- Feeling hopeless
- Having no reason to live
- Being a burden to others
- Feeling trapped
- Unbearable pain

Continue on next page:

----

[9] https://afsp.org/about-suicide/risk-factors-and-warning-signs/

<u>American Foundation for Suicide Prevention</u>
<u>Suicide Warning Signs</u>[9]

Continued:

Behaviors that may signal risk, especially if related to a painful event, loss or change:
- Increased use of alcohol or drugs
- Looking for a way to end their lives, such as searching online for materials or means
- Withdrawing from activities
- Isolating from family and friends
- Sleeping too much or too little
- Visiting or calling people to say goodbye
- Giving away prized possessions
- Aggression
- Fatigue

More information can be found on the website of American Foundation for Suicide Prevention at <u>www.afsp.org.</u>

PARENTS

Become a True Power Parent!

Go to
www.MaryLynneFernandez.com
to learn more.

Parents & Organization Leaders:

As a certified life coach, keynote speaker, and author, Mary Lynne is a sought-after personal empowerment leader of parents of teenagers.

She speaks and connects deeply with both teen and adult audiences. Using her own life experiences, she inspires and fulfills your desire and need to understand the teenage world.

Mary Lynne is available to speak at your event virtually or in person!

As a coach, she offers programs for parents to end personal and family conflict so they can have more connection and less confrontation with their teenager.

"I loved Mary Lynne's positive attitude, she's so creative and open on a personal level. My biggest take-away from this presentation and workshop is that I now recognize my positive attributes. As a result of this presentation, I will pursue my goals without doubt."
— Teenage boy

"Outgoing and expressive! Mary Lynne has good stage presence using motion and questions to keep everyone interested. She was even able to deal with random audience distractions without losing focus."
— Youth organization

"I discovered myself and what my true happiness is."
— Teenage girl

"Mary Lynne's presentation was very inspiring. I really related to her story which helped me to see what I can become and all the other possibilities."
— Teenage boy

"My 3 teenage boys attended a group class offered by Mary Lynne. The boys were very responsive to the themes of creating goals and steps necessary to achieve them. My 16-year old particularly called upon the things he learned as he prepared for finishing high school and planning for college. In our case, enabling our kids to start thinking about their future (and present) allowed them to become more mature and they began to advocate for themselves."
— Parent

"My youngest son did individual Life Coaching with Mary Lynne during the school year. We've always known he's a smart kid but he always seemed to be behind on things. Mary Lynne worked with him twice a week on formulating a plan for tracking his assignments, tests, and due dates. He learned how to study more effectively and how to stay organized no matter how busy he was. He became less overwhelmed and more consistently prepared then he had been previously. I tried on numerous occasions to work with him on the same things and for whatever reason, we always ended up in an argument."

— Parent

"My husband and I attended a parenting class Mary Lynne directed, which provided so much valuable information about dealing with our four teenage kids. As a result, we were able to show them the kind of respect that helped them rise to the occasion and make more of their own choices with confidence. The practice techniques helped us to implement changes in our household that stuck, even in day to day situations."

— Parent

"As an event planner, working with Mary Lynne was awesome. She was quick to respond, interested in our situation, and open to ideas and thoughts. She was also thorough in providing information and details on her end. I cannot wait to have her back to present again."

— Youth Organization Event Planner

Acknowledgements

Thank you to all those who have impacted my life - I have learned so much from each and every one of you. Thank you, Mom & Dad, for all that you have done for me and taught me. Thank you to all my students and clients for teaching me many life lessons. Thank you to my spiritual teachers for leading me back to my heart. Thank you, Chico, for your endless support and adventures together. Thank you, Liz, Keli, and Susan for checking in during my writing process. Thank you, Tom Bird, for teaching me how to write and access the writer within myself. Thank you, Desiree Phillips, for your support through the writing process. Thank you, John Hodgkinson. You are the book publishing and social media marketing guru! I am very appreciative of all your help and support. Thank you, Gagan Sarkaria. Words cannot express the appreciation I have for your encouragement, support, healing, and wise teachings. You have supported and guided me to completely transform my life as I have worked through many of my own barriers. I am deeply grateful for all that you have helped me with, personally and professionally. You are a special person and friend to me. Thanks to you and Abbey Wilkerson, I have the best book cover ever! Thank you both for all your help with the development, design, and creation of it. Thank you, Meghan, Mr. Freeland and your CGHS students, Annette (Kaity & Nick), Gladys and family, Jo and kids, and Desiree & Morgan for your feedback during the cover design phase. Most importantly, thank you to my Higher Power for leading me down this path and always having my back! I am forever grateful.

About the Author

Mary Lynne Fernandez is a successful keynote speaker, transformational life coach, and an insightful business consultant. She brings forth over 14 years of enthusiastic expertise in the field of coaching young adults while profoundly empowering their parents. She has passionately served tweens, teens, and their parents as a middle school teacher and as a life coach. To every client, audience, project, and challenge, Mary Lynne brings forth fairness, humility, and gratitude. Her kind and honest style of speaking and coaching have earned her immense respect and love in her community.

Mary Lynne Fernandez struggled during her teenage years like so many teens do today. She overcame the struggle and teaches others to do the same. Today she is respected as a powerhouse "Teen-Esteem Expert."

With depression and suicide being a part of Mary Lynne's past, she helps break barriers by being real and educating on both topics. Using her own life experiences, she inspires and fulfills the desire and need to understand the teenage world and to overcome personal life struggles in order to have self-love and family connection.

Mary Lynne lives in Colorado with her husband and two Australian Shepherd dogs. She enjoys traveling, skiing, swimming, hiking, biking, and playing tennis.